My Perfect

Imperfections

Jalpa Williby

This edition published via CreateSpace

My Perfect Imperfections
All Rights Reserved.
Copyright © 2015 Jalpa Williby
ISBN: 1515224740
ISBN-13: 978-1515224747

Edited by: Maureen E. Angell, Ph.D. and Angie Martin
Formatted by: Angie Martin
Cover by: Amanda Walker

To learn more about Jalpa Williby and her works,
please visit her website: http://jalpawilliby.com.

Books by Jalpa Williby

<u>The Chaysing Series</u>

Chaysing Dreams (Book 1)

Chaysing Memories (Book 2)

Chaysing Destiny (Book 3)

Cerebral Palsy: My Perfect Imperfections

(coming soon)

(Nonfiction companion book for

My Perfect Imperfections)

Dedication

My Perfect Imperfections is dedicated to all of the angels

who have crossed my path.

Thank you for your inspiration.

Thank you for sharing your wisdom.

Prologue

"Congratulations! You have beautiful little girls. Oh, and, by the way, one of the twins has Cerebral Palsy."

I always wondered how the doctors broke the news to my parents about my diagnosis. I used to visualize the entire scenario.

"What are you talking about, Doctor? What does that even mean?" I could picture my mom asking, her eyes filling with tears.

"Well, is this curable? What is the prognosis?" Dad would ask, always the practical one, looking for answers.

"I know this is a lot to take in. It's a neurological disorder. There are things we can do to help. Lily can go through intense physical, occupational, and speech therapy. Actually, she'll probably need therapy most of her life. I have pamphlets I can give you…and you can read information about Cerebral Palsy. Oh, and I can give you references to some really great support groups. I mean, you'll be surprised how many parents have to go through this type of thing." The doctor would ramble on and on, never really answering the questions directly.

Dad probably became angry, his voice getting louder. "Look, Doc, I just asked if she's going to get better. That's all I want to know!"

Mom most likely started crying quietly to herself, knowing in her heart why the doctor was vague. I could see both being left with more questions than answers, fearing their lives had just turned upside down.

My name is Elizabeth Skye Cooper. Well, most people just call me Lily. I am eighteen years old, and I have Cerebral Palsy. What exactly is Cerebral Palsy? According to Webster, it is "a disability resulting from damage to the brain before, during, or shortly after birth and outwardly manifested by muscular incoordination and speech disturbances."

Blah, blah, blah. I hate stupid definitions.

I'll tell you what I know of Cerebral Palsy. It sucks. I can't move my body the way I want to move it. I'm mostly confined to my wheelchair because I can't walk without assistance. I can't even feed myself since my arm is not able to bring the damn food to my mouth because of my inability to coordinate my muscles. I know what I want my arm to do, but it won't cooperate no matter how hard I try. Didn't I tell you it sucks?

I've lived with it for eighteen years, and nobody understands my body more than I do. None of those doctors, none of those therapists, not even my family. Through the years, I've learned to make the most of it. I can actually drive my wheelchair and talk with my communication device.

It hasn't been easy. No, it hasn't been easy.

Facing the World

Reality

JALPA WILLIBY

4

Chapter One

T he rain slamming on the windshield is making it impossible to
see clearly. I can tell she's too upset to notice that she's driving
too fast, especially around the curves. I bite my bottom lip and
swallow the scream from escaping when the van slips a few times. I
don't want to yell at her for fear that she'll turn around to check on
me while driving. Instead, I hold my breath and pray that she'll slow
down.

The headlights come from nowhere, blinding us. Where did
they come from?

"Hold on, Lily!" she yells as she spins the steering wheel.

My heart stops beating when the van swerves out of control.
I shut my eyes as the deafening sound of the screeching brakes and
the crunching metal hits me like a tidal wave. The shattered glass
tinkles around me, and everything moves in slow motion. As our van
continues to spin, a deathly silence encases me.

I hear nothing. I feel nothing. I'm floating...and my life
flashes before my eyes.

When I was much younger, I used think that I was just like the other
kids. I didn't even realize I was different. Sure, my parents took me
to a lot of therapy sessions, but I just figured all kids attended classes
like these. It didn't really register until much later that my twin sister,
Layna, never attended those sessions with me.

I suspected I was different when I was about four years old. I
still remember that day. My mom brought Layna and me to a park

because it was spring, and the weather was especially nice that day. Layna had run off to the other side of the park to play on the slide.

While I was sitting in my wheelchair, this little girl, Sara—yes, I still remember her name—skipped toward me and asked me to play tag. She kept pulling on my hand to get out of my wheelchair.

"Come on, come play with me," she insisted.

"Sara, no, honey. She can't play with you," her mom said, trying to tug her daughter away, looking uneasy. She barely glanced my way.

I wanted to use my words, too. I wanted to tell Sara that I'd like to play with her, but I couldn't talk like her. The words just wouldn't come out even though, in my mind, I was thinking them.

"Sara, this is Lily. Maybe you two can swing together? I can hold Lily on a swing next to you," my mom suggested, her voice sounding overly cheerful. This clearly meant my mom was becoming uncomfortable with the situation.

"Oh, we were just leaving, anyway," Sara's mom interjected. "It was nice to meet you. Take care." With that, Sara's mom picked her up and rushed away.

That was the first time I noticed that people acted differently around me. I could tell Sara's mom was uncomfortable and couldn't wait to get away from us. In hindsight, I suppose similar events occurred prior to this one, but I was just too young to notice. Besides, most of the time, Layna talked for me, so I never sensed anything was wrong.

I convinced myself that once people got used to me and got to know me, they wouldn't act so awkward around me.

I was wrong.

Mom decided to be a stay-at-home mom so she could take care of us. Dad worked long hours to help pay for all of the medical bills. As far as I was concerned, life was good. So what that they had to carry me, take me to the bathroom, feed me, and basically do everything for me? I had their undivided attention. Yep, life was good.

As Layna and I were growing up, I often wondered why she

didn't need a wheelchair like me. Okay, a part of me was hoping she would have the same problems as me. I knew it was stupid to think that way, but hey, at least I was honest.

I could tell Layna was completely different from me. While I was placed on the floor to move as I willed, Layna would crawl all over me. I couldn't even get on my hands and knees, let alone move around the room like her.

When I realized that she could move much better than I could, I wanted to hate her. I was actually jealous of how much more she could do compared to me. While I was learning to walk small steps in my therapy sessions with the help of the therapist and my braces, Layna was running around all over the place. She was free to do whatever she wanted, without anybody helping her. It wasn't fair! Oh, how I wanted to hate her.

But, Layna wouldn't allow it. She just had too much love to give. She was always attached to me. If I was lying on the floor mat while Mom stretched me, Layna would put her head on my tummy and hug tightly. As soon as she was able to push my wheelchair, she would take me from one room to another, making sure I didn't get bored.

One night, Layna woke up sobbing. We must have been no more than five years old. No matter how hard my parents tried to calm her down, she wouldn't stop. She was hysterical, and she refused to tell my parents anything.

While lying in my bed listening to Layna, I started to become upset. I could hear her crying from the next room. Was she hurting? Was she sick? Even though I tried to fight the tears, they seemed to sneak out. Finally, it all got to be too much. I couldn't control my own crying, and I eventually reached a point where I was bawling just as loud as Layna.

My dad came running into my room. "Lily, what's wrong? Are you hurting? What's wrong?" His frantic eyes were anxiously searching for some type of reassurance from me.

In between my sobs, I looked at the door, pointing with my arm. He must have figured out that I was worried about Layna because he said, "Layna is fine. Don't worry about her. She probably just had a bad dream."

That answer wasn't good enough for me. I cried even louder.

In his panic, Dad yelled for Mom. She came running in with Layna in her arms.

"What's happening? Is everything okay in here?" Mom's face was pale, looking beaten down.

"I think she's worried about Layna," Dad explained.

"Oh, honey. Don't worry about her. She's just upset, that's all." Mom tried to keep her voice soft. She put Layna down so I could see for myself.

As soon as Layna saw me, she ran to me, screaming hysterically. When she crawled into my bed, I reached out to touch her. To my surprise, Layna calmed down as she wrapped her arms around me. Still gasping for air while she tried to settle herself down, Layna soon fell asleep, cuddled next to me.

Both my parents stared at the interaction in awe. Slowly, they tip-toed out of my room.

Layna continued to sleep in my room from that night on, and that was the start of our unbreakable bond. Layna became my best friend.

I finally started walking around the age of four when I took my first steps in the walker with my physical therapist, Julie. It was a special walker that rolled behind me, and since I couldn't hold the walker with my hands, my arms were stabilized by a platform attached to the walker. It was called a posterior platform rolling walker. Julie had been working with me on getting my leg muscles strong enough to bear weight. She placed me in the walker, and my parents were there, along with Layna, to cheer me on.

This was a big deal to me because I had never walked without anybody holding me. In this special walker, the goal was for me to take steps on my own. It was very stressful because I wanted to show off to my parents.

I think they sensed my uneasiness because Mom said, "It's going to be fine, Lily. Just do your best. We're very proud of you."

Dad was a bit sterner. "Lily, I want you to give it your all. You've been working hard, so this is the time to shine."

Wow, thanks, Dad, for putting even more pressure on me.

Once positioned with the walker, Julie told me to try to move my legs forward as if walking. I stared down at my legs and willed them to move. Some signal went from my brain down to my right leg and I saw it being lifted up. Somehow it came forward. Then I did the same with my left leg. I couldn't believe it! My legs were moving! Okay, they weren't perfect steps. As a matter of fact, my feet were sort of tripping over each other, and my knees were bent. Even though I had braces for my feet, it looked like I was still walking on my toes. They may not be perfect steps, but all I cared about was that I was walking. Nothing could take the smile of joy off my face!

My dad praised me, jumping up and down, while my mom cried tears of joy. But, nobody cheered for me louder than Layna. It was as if I had just won the Olympics.

Through the years, I held on to special moments of triumph such as these.

❧❧❧

Growing up, while Layna attended dance lessons, I attended my therapy sessions. Mom and Dad would take turns driving us around to our appointments. I knew it was hard on them because there were times when we'd hear them yelling at each other about how they were going to get us where we needed to be. It was always very stressful when they got into their fights. Layna and I would stay quiet, staring at each other, both of us praying that it would end soon. We knew that when they fought, the rest of the day would be ruined. They'd avoid talking to one another and have permanent frowns on their foreheads.

Usually, as soon as I would reach my therapy sessions, I'd forget about the incidents. As hard as it was for me to work, I really enjoyed the sessions. It was one place where I felt like I almost fit in. Well, sort of. There were other kids there like me, so I didn't feel out of place. The therapists were really great, too. It was refreshing that they talked to me like they'd talk to any other kid. They expected me to work when I was with them. They didn't baby me. Instead, they pushed my body to exhaustion. I liked it, though, because I felt accomplished.

Julie, my physical therapist, would even work with me in the pool. That was the best. I could actually feel my muscles relax, and it was so much easier to walk in there. I felt like I was even able to support my weight.

Although I did enjoy my therapy sessions, I hated the multiple surgeries I had to have. My muscles were becoming tighter, and I had to have surgeries to cut my heel cords, inner thigh muscles, and hamstrings. Then they would put me in a cast for a long time. It would get very hot with these casts, and they would keep me immobilized.

I guess I can whine and complain about my life, but at the end of the day, I had to face reality. This was my life, and it wasn't going to change anytime soon.

Sometimes, if I had great therapy sessions, the therapists would let me leave early. I loved those days because I'd make it in time to watch Layna practice. I used to love watching her dance. She was like an angel with her long, blonde hair and blue eyes. I could watch her forever. We were as opposite as can be. While she had long, curly, blonde hair with blue eyes, I had wavy, dark hair with green eyes.

When I would watch her at one of her recitals as she conquered that dance floor, I would imagine getting out of my wheelchair and walking toward her. Then, I would imagine both of us performing the routines together—Layna with her beautiful, blonde hair flowing, and I would dance just as gracefully next to her with my long, dark hair. We would be known as the dancing sisters.

Of course, that never happened. It only was real in my head.

But, imagination could be a beautiful thing. After all, I could imagine anything I wanted. I may have no control over my physical body. I may be dependent on others to take care of me, but at least the imagination was mine. Nobody could take that away from me.

Besides, it was my imagination and my dreams that kept me sane on most days.

Chapter Two

S ince I wasn't able to talk well, my speech therapist trained me to use a communication device. It was great because I could control the device with my eyes using an eye scanning method. If what I wanted to say wasn't programmed into the device, I had the option of typing out my sentences. At first, this was very hard and time consuming. Eventually, though, I got so good with using it that I could actually hold a conversation with somebody. The device had word predictions, phrases, and even sentences. This helped speed it up for me. I compared it to Layna texting with her phone. The more she texted—and trust me, it was all the time—the faster she got. I would be amazed at how fast her thumbs worked. She would simply say that the fact that I could do the same thing with my eyes was even more amazing. Truth be told, the communication device was my lifesaver. I could actually communicate my wants and needs.

It would be extremely frustrating if I didn't have my communication device accessible to me. Sometimes, they'd forget to make it available for me at school, which was really annoying. I mean, imagine if somebody's voice was taken away from them for the day. What if they had to use the bathroom, and they couldn't even ask for help? So, when they'd forget to make my device available to me, I learned to yell to get their attention. I learned that if I threw enough fuss, they would eventually realize that I needed my communication device to tell them my needs.

Now, don't get me wrong. I could communicate simple things. For example, I could look up for yes and down for no. I could even point toward something either by looking in that direction or moving my arm that way. I could always drive my wheelchair to where I wanted. I was able to say a few simple words, although my speech was pretty difficult to understand. Besides, like I said, if all else failed, yelling to get somebody's attention worked every time.

My other lifesaver was my wheelchair. I was able to control my left arm better, so I learned to drive it with a joystick placed on my left side. This gave me independence with my mobility. If I wanted to remove myself from a particular area or a situation, I simply drove away. I couldn't even imagine being stuck in a place that I didn't want to be and wait for others to move me.

Out of all of the people in my life, nobody knew me better than Layna. Not even my parents. It was almost like she could read my mind. I'd just had to make a certain face, and she knew what I was thinking. Many times, she was my savior.

Slowly, I learned to make the best of my disabilities—and, more importantly, my abilities.

One of the first lessons I learned in life was that good things usually didn't last forever.

I was eight years old at the time, and it was Christmas morning. While I was sitting in my wheelchair, Layna was bringing my gifts to me and helping me open them one at a time. I noticed Dad sneaking away, but returning quickly. Layna squealed in delight when she noticed the beautiful puppy in his arms. The black Labrador leaped off and sprinted toward Layna and me. Both of us couldn't stop laughing as the puppy was jumping around in front of us. Layna picked him up and brought him to me. When he started kissing my face all over, I knew instantly that he was going to be my best buddy.

"Is he for us, Daddy?" Layna asked the question I was thinking. I couldn't believe the puppy was ours.

"He sure is. You can name him whatever you want!"

"Really? What do you want to name him, Lily?" Layna turned to him while patting the puppy as he sat in my lap.

I placed my arm on him so I could feel his fur under my hand. Although it was hard for me to have a smooth, controlled movement with my arms, I focused extra hard to gently touch the puppy. I didn't want him to be startled and scared of me.

After thinking about it for a few moments, I used my

communication device and said, "How about Duke?"

Layna smiled. "I love it!"

There were several reasons why I wanted to name him Duke. First of all, he looked like Duke to me. Secondly, the "d" sound was easier for me to express. So even if I couldn't say his full name, "Duke," I knew I could at least make the sound "Du."

Once I started trying to say his name, he quickly figured out that I was calling for him. Every time I said, "Du," he'd lift his head to me and slobber all over my face. I remembered the feeling of pure bliss that somebody was actually responding to me calling their name.

Unfortunately, our happiness didn't last too long that Christmas. The next day while we were all eating breakfast, Mom and Dad dropped the bomb on us. They said that they had decided to get a divorce.

"You know we'll always love you, and we're always here for you two," Mom said, avoiding eye contact.

I didn't know exactly what "divorce" actually meant, but I knew several kids from school whose parents also had gotten divorced. From the way my stomach knotted up, I had a feeling that it was not a good thing.

"You're not going to be married anymore?" Layna asked, her voice shaky.

"Now, Layna, you must understand that this does not affect Lily and you at all. I will always be your daddy and your mother will always be your mommy." Dad reached out to hold her hand, but Layna quickly snatched it away.

"Why?" I asked with my device.

Both stayed quiet for a few seconds. Mom finally sighed and said, "Honey, sometimes things don't go as planned. You just have to know that no matter what happens with your daddy and me, our relationship with you two will never change."

Suddenly, all of the guilt that I had carried for the past ten years of my life began to resurface. I didn't want to lose it in front of them. I shut them out and hid in my safe world by bringing my head down and not responding. I simply didn't want to hear any more.

"Lily, please don't do this. It's important to talk about your feelings now," Mom said, trying to keep her voice soft. I knew her too well, though, because I could already hear her voice trembling.

"Leave her alone, Jackie," Dad said. "Can't you see she needs time to deal with this?"

"Really, Bill? I'm trying to help her. You see that she's upset, right?"

By then, I just wanted to get away from them. Layna must have wanted the same thing because without saying a word, she took my wheelchair and pushed it into our bedroom.

It was nice that we still shared the same room. After Duke ran into the room behind us, she slammed the door and locked it. Plopping herself on her bed, she stared at me.

I frantically began using my communication device. "Do you think this is my fault? Maybe they're getting a divorce because of me."

"Why would you think that, Lily?" Layna asked, confused.

"The stress of taking care of me. They always have to do things for me." By then, I couldn't hold back the tears.

"Lily, don't cry. What you're saying makes no sense. They'll still be taking care of us. They're our parents, so that's not going to change." Layna got up and wiped my tears from my face.

I got myself so worked up by then that I couldn't even hold my head steady to talk with my device. Instead, I just sat in my wheelchair and sobbed, letting the guilt swallow me.

Duke began howling, sensing that something was terribly wrong. Layna knew there was nothing she could do for me. She knew I needed some time to cry it all out. She gave me my space and held my hand until I was done with my breakdown.

"Sorry," I finally replied.

"It's fine, Lily. Let them do what they want. Who cares? At least we'll always have each other. I'll never leave you."

Chapter Three

The divorce went through fast. Soon after, Layna and I got used to our new routine. We both stayed with Mom in our home, and Dad moved a few towns over. He still helped with taking us to our appointments and events, but he just didn't stay in the same house as us. Luckily, he made sure his new house was wheelchair accessible, so I was able to visit him every other weekend.

Although Layna and I were still upset with our parents going through with the divorce, we knew there wasn't much we could do about it. Adults were just weird.

Duke was very protective of Layna and me. It was unbelievable how intelligent he was. He was always gentle with me, but played rough with Layna. Before and after school, all three of us would go for a walk. I would drive my power wheelchair while Layna would hold Duke's leash to walk him. I loved these walks because I felt free and independent. I cherished this quiet time with the two beings I loved the most in this world. More importantly, both loved me for who I was. I could be completely myself around them without worrying about being judged.

As I got older, I learned to tolerate the long days at school. For example, I learned to ignore the discomfort from sitting in the wheelchair for such long periods of time. It's the worst feeling in the world not being able to even shift my weight in the wheelchair. So many times, I just wanted to be able to stand up for a few seconds to stretch my legs and relieve the pressure from my butt. Instead, I learned to deal with it, just like everything else.

Nobody said life was going to be easy—especially for a girl like me.

When we started high school, I admit I was intimidated. I was used to being bullied. It got so bad at times in middle school that I would cry as soon as I came home. There were kids who would imitate the way I tried to talk or the way my body moved.

Once they realized that I was Layna's sister, though, they'd back off. Layna was well known and liked. It just wouldn't look good to be on Layna's bad side.

I knew I had to deal with the new kids in high school who didn't know Layna or me. That first day of class, I was very overwhelmed. There were too many kids standing and walking through the hallways. Luckily, I was pretty good at driving my wheelchair, so I wasn't worried about running into anybody. Most of my classes were with the "normal" kids because I've always had an above average intelligence. That was never the problem. Still, there were some classes I attended that were segregated with the special needs kids.

Although I was scared at first, I soon realized that it was just like any other school I had attended. The kids didn't even notice me. While I was driving my wheelchair, I didn't even get a "hi" from anybody. As a matter of fact, it was like I wasn't there. These kids just looked right through me.

I guess it would have been easier to feel invisible. Instead, I felt painfully visible, but entirely ignored.

Although I was challenged physically, I was easily able to keep up with the "normal" kids intellectually. I could read, spell, do math, and type with my communication device. My biggest drawback was my physical limitation. Even my speech was severely affected. I could say a few words fairly clearly, but generally, my speech was difficult to understand.

If people didn't know me, they usually assumed that I was affected cognitively as well. At first, it used to bother me, but by the time I was in high school, I expected it. They would talk to me as if they were talking to a toddler.

Layna had programmed my device to say, "Yes, I have Cerebral Palsy. And, yes, I can have normal conversations with you." I pressed this button quite a bit just to check the ignorant people.

I was thankful that although I couldn't control my body, at least I had my mind. Even if physically I continued to decline slowly as I was getting older, at least my mind continued to be sharp.

Yes, the truth of the matter was that as my body was growing, it was harder for me to control my muscles. For example, it was much more challenging to stand and walk. Luckily, I was still able to do it with assistance, but it was much easier when my body was smaller.

I was also thankful that I could still use the toilet and was able to eat regular foods. Sure, somebody had to help clean me after I used the toilet, help feed me and bathe me, but I learned to focus on the positives. At least I didn't have to wear diapers, and I was still able to enjoy the taste of food.

I would hang on to that as long as I possibly could.

I was used to my routine. Most days, I was a happy girl. I always looked forward to coming home and hanging out with Layna and Duke in the evenings. Although I normally kept a smile on my face, occasionally there were days when things just felt bleak. I had no friends besides Layna. Sure, her friends were nice to me whenever they came over, but they weren't my friends. Sometimes, I would even find myself being jealous of Layna doing her "girly" things with her friends.

She was always very good with including me. Knowing Layna, she would have it no other way. If she was having people over for a sleepover, I would be right there with them. If she was having a movie night, she would even take me with her. At times, I did feel guilty about it. I didn't want to hold her back from her social life. But, the selfish part of me—the part that didn't want Layna to have an independent life away from me—kept tagging along.

One day, Layna was asked to her homecoming dance by a cute boy she had a crush on. Timmy had stopped by the house a few times, and he was always very nice. This was going to be Layna's first dance with a boy. She was beyond excited.

"Can you believe he asked me, Lily? He was so cute when he asked! I mean, he was very shy. He barely could look at me when he gave me the roses." Layna was in her own glory. Timmy had given her the dozen roses by her locker at school.

I couldn't stop laughing as she explained every detail of how he had asked her. I adored Timmy, and to see Layna this happy made me happy. After reliving this moment with her for the hundredth time—because I'm sure she must have told me the story at least that much—I started wondering if I was ever going to get asked for a dance.

Layna must have sensed the shift in my mood because immediately she asked what was wrong.

I smiled and with my device, I replied, "Nothing. Just tired."

"I know you too well, and I always know when you're lying. What's wrong, Lily?"

We were both in the kitchen, so I tried to drive away from her. I certainly did not want her to feel bad for going to her dance because of me. Layna felt bad about everything when it came to me. She would change her whole life around just to make sure I was happy. I hated the way that made me feel.

She followed me to our room. "Come on, Lily. You tell me everything. What's the matter?"

I took a deep breath, knowing that she was not going to stop until I talked with her. "I wonder sometimes if I will ever go to any dances."

"Of course, you are, silly!"

I frantically typed with my device. "Layna, who would ask me? Look at me! Have you noticed anything different about me?"

Layna stared at me for a few moments. Finally, she said, "Lily, you do know how perfect you are, right?"

This was always what got me mad about her. Why did she say stupid things like that? "Stop!" I said with my device. "Please leave me alone."

She didn't stop. "If people don't see how perfect you are, they're stupid. They don't see what I see, Lily. You are beautiful. Besides that, you are one of the strongest girls I know! Look at you!"

"Yeah, look at me. People have to take care of me, Layna. *You* have to take care of me. You give me baths every day…feed me. You even have to wipe me after I use the bathroom!" By then, I was becoming very frustrated.

"Yet, you always keep a smile on your face. Lily, you inspire me every day. Don't you know you're an angel? One day, a gorgeous guy is going to see what I see, and he will treat you like a princess." Layna gave me a hug. "Hold on, I want you to dance with me right now. I'm going to play this song that reminds me of you." She pulled her iPhone out. After a few moments, the song, *Perfect* by Pink began to play.

Layna took my hands and sang the lyrics at the top of her lungs. She danced while holding my hands around the wheelchair. Duke also jumped around with her, wanting to be in on the fun. It was all so cute that I couldn't help but laugh with her.

So I danced. I danced with my sister. While she sang the words to the song, I sang with her...yelled at the top of my lungs.

From that day on, whenever either of us was having a rough day, we would play that song, dance with each other, and sing our own version.

Chapter Four

Layna made a lot of friends in high school, especially since she made the varsity dance team. Besides that, she was beautiful and excelled in all classes. The meeting place for all of the "popular kids" eventually became where my locker was located because Layna was always by my locker waiting for me. It felt really good to finally have some friends. Well, they were really Layna's friends, but it didn't matter. I liked being right in the center of everything. They were kind of cool, too, because sometimes they'd even include me in their conversations.

Layna walked me every day to most of my classes whenever she could, making sure I arrived safely. Even though I could easily drive to classes independently, I didn't complain. Just being around Layna's positive energy kept me in my happy place.

Once, when Layna was walking me to my life skills class, which was specific for special needs kids, there were two boys walking in front of us. They must have been freshmen because they seemed to be searching for their classes since it was the start of a new year.

One of the guys grabbed the other one and said, "No, not that classroom, dude. That's the retarded classroom."

The other boy laughed.

I was used to comments like that, but Layna was not going to let it slide. I could tell by the way she raised her chin up and squared her shoulders.

"Excuse me?" Layna marched right up to them.

Both boys turned beet red, recognizing Layna instantly. Now that we were juniors, everybody knew her. Immediately, they noticed me in my wheelchair next to her. I almost felt sorry for them because they looked humiliated. They did not want to get on the bad side of the most popular girl in school.

"Err, sorry…we didn't mean…" The boy appeared flustered and embarrassed.

"What exactly did you mean? Have you even tried to get to know anybody from this class? Oh, and meet my sister. This is Lily. I'm pretty sure she can kick both of your butts when it comes to any IQ tests."

I couldn't help but smile. Layna knew exactly how smart I was.

"Sorry," the other boy mumbled, staring at the floor.

A small crowd had gathered around, curious about the commotion.

Mrs. Torres, my teacher, stepped out. "What's going on, ladies?"

"Oh, nothing we can't handle, Mrs. Torres. I've come to realize that some humans are born just to occupy space." Layna glared one more time at the boys, who continued to look ashamed. "Come on, Lily. They've already taken more of our time than they deserve."

When Layna walked me to my desk, I gave her a high five. Then, we both giggled in victory.

Growing up, we never had money, so we rarely could take any vacations outside of going to waterparks occasionally. For that reason, Layna and I were especially surprised when Mom said we were going camping for the weekend.

"Really, Mom? We've never gone camping. Are we going to know what to do?" Layna asked.

"Dad's coming with us," Mom answered quickly.

What? Dad's coming with us? That's a bit strange. I mean Dad was always in the picture, but why would he go on a vacation with us?

"Who's all going, Mom?" Layna asked, now curious.

"You, Lily, Duke, Dad, and I," Mom replied, like it was the most natural thing in the world.

Layna didn't say anything more about it to Mom, but when we were alone, she asked, "What do you think about Dad going with us?

Don't you think it's strange? I mean, it's a family vacation. Wouldn't it be awesome if they got back together?"

Using my device, I answered, "Don't jump to conclusions. He's probably just coming along to help us out."

"I don't know, Lily. Neither of them has dated anybody seriously after the divorce. Think about it."

I guess Layna had a point, but I had learned through the years not to get my hopes up high for anything.

Friday evening, Dad drove the van to the campgrounds about three hours away. The site was large enough, so our camping spot was nice and private. He put up two tents. They had brought the lightweight manual wheelchair for me, so he carried me out and placed me in it. He set up sleeping bags in both tents and then built a fire. Duke ran around us, excited to be out in nature.

"Isn't this great, girls? We're going to have a blast! A real family time," Dad said as the fire came to life.

"It's perfect, Bill," Mom said, smiling.

Layna came by me and whispered, "Let's see which tent Mom sleeps in tonight."

After eating dinner and singing some songs by the fire, it was already dark, so Dad carried me to the tent. He tucked me into my sleeping bag and gave me a kiss on my forehead. "Goodnight, munchkin. Sweet dreams and I love you."

I vocalized I loved him, too. Of course, it sounded like I was just making noise, but Dad knew exactly what I was saying to him. When Layna walked into the tent, he hugged her and told her he loved her as well.

When he left, Layna slipped into her own sleeping bag. "See, I told you! They're sharing the same tent, Lily!" she whispered, her voice full of excitement.

I couldn't help but laugh. As much as I didn't want to get my hopes up, a part of me still wished that they'd get back together. For a brief moment, I allowed myself to dream of this.

After listening to Layna talk about school, dancing, and boys, I finally fell asleep.

The next morning, Mom and Dad seemed especially happy. I even caught him caressing Mom's back at times. Layna would throw her knowing looks in my direction whenever she saw them being affectionate.

That afternoon, Dad suggested a hike. Since it would be difficult to push the wheelchair through the trails, it was decided that Dad, Duke, and Layna would go hiking. Mom and I would stay by the tent. I didn't mind. I was just happy to be out in the sun and feeling the breeze combing through my hair.

After an hour of Mom reading her book while I listened to music, she approached me to check on me. "How are you doing, Lily? Do you want to get down and stretch for a while?"

I shook my head no. I was feeling very peaceful, and I didn't want the feeling to end.

"I've had an upset stomach all day. I feel like I need to use the bathroom again. Would you mind if I go try to do that? I won't be too far, and I should be back within minutes."

Again, I shook my head no. I knew Mom was having stomach issues.

"Okay, I'll be right back," Mom said, squeezing my hand.

I watched her walk into the woods until she finally disappeared from sight. Since there were no toilets around, they just used the woods. They did bring the adapted, portable commode for me, though. There would be no way my body could squat to the ground.

As I waited for Mom, I closed my eyes, cherishing the serenity that was spreading over me.

Within minutes, I sensed something was wrong. When my eyes flew open, I saw a dog across the clearing. When I squinted my eyes for a better view, I suddenly realized it was a wolf. And, this wolf was staring right at me.

My heart sank from fear. I wanted to scream, run, and yell for help. *Oh my god, what am I going to do?*

I turned my head toward the direction Mom had disappeared, but I didn't see her. If I had my power wheelchair, maybe I could have done something like try to drive away from here. Instead, I was stuck, helpless, in this manual wheelchair, waiting for my fate.

The wolf slowly strolled toward me, and to my dismay, his fangs were out.

God, if you're there, and this is how I'm going to leave this world, please make it quick. Please don't make me suffer.

I looked down when he was about ten feet away from me. I didn't want to look at him straight in his eyes because I read somewhere that if you look in their eyes, they may feel threatened. I didn't understand what he wanted from me. I had nothing for him, not even food. Why was he stalking me?

As the hand of fear gripped my throat, I closed my eyes. I had no courage to keep them open. I could hear him sniffing around me. Why was this happening? Where was Mom? Completely frozen from fear, his hot breath fanned my face. He was sniffing me, but I dared not open my eyes. Feeling lightheaded, with tremors running through my body, I felt the air around me go completely still. Although it must have been mere seconds, it felt like my life flashed before my eyes. Bracing myself for the attack, a lonely tear rolled down my face. I was suddenly shocked when I felt his wet tongue on my cheek where the tear had left its trail. I wanted to turn my head away, but again, I remained motionless.

Soon, I no longer felt him next to me. What happened? Although still terrified to open my eyes, I slowly forced myself to sneak a peek.

The wolf was gone.

I glanced around, stunned. Then I spotted him. He was sitting by the tree line, watching me. Why was he still here? What did he want? But, I dared not move.

Shortly, I heard Mom's footsteps. Oh no, the wolf would attack her! What could I do? I looked at her frantically, hoping she'd figure out that she was in danger. As soon as she saw the fear in my face, she immediately knew something was wrong.

Within seconds she reached me. "What's wrong? What happened, Lily?"

I threw my head toward the direction of the wolf. Mom turned her head to face the wolf, who was now standing up, watching us. Her grip tightened around my shoulders briefly, and she positioned herself in front of me. The wolf watched us for few more seconds, and then miraculously, turned to disappear into the woods.

Mom and I didn't move as the shock of what just happened sank in. When Mom was satisfied that he was gone, she turned to me.

"Oh my god, Lily. Are you okay?" She quickly examined me. When she noticed the footsteps made by the wolf around my wheelchair, she knew what had happened. "What the...he came all the way to you, Lily?"

I nodded, trembling with fear.

Mom grabbed her cell phone and called Dad. "Bill, you have to get back here. There was a wolf here." She started crying into the phone. "Please hurry."

Dad, Layna, and Duke were back within half an hour. All three were panting, so I had a feeling they all ran back.

"What happened?" Dad asked, frantic.

Mom began shaking. "A wolf was here. He left now. I had to use the bathroom. Bill, he came right by Lily. Oh my god, he was right next to Lily." Mom was hysterical as she rambled.

"I don't know what you're saying. Where were you when he was by Lily?" Dad asked, coming to me and picking me out of the wheelchair, holding me in his embrace. I could feel him trembling as well.

"I wasn't here, Bill. Remember, I said I've had an upset stomach all day. I stepped away just for a few moments. And—"

"You left Lily?" Dad turned to her. He placed me back into the wheelchair.

Layna came to me and grabbed my hand. She asked me if I was okay with her eyes. I nodded, not wanting her to worry.

"Bill, it was for a few moments only," Mom tried to explain.

"Are you crazy? How could you leave her alone? She's defenseless. Imagine how she must have felt!" Dad was screaming at her. "You have no common sense. Never did! No wonder we got a divorce. Probably the best decision I ever made!" Dad was being very cruel by then.

"That's not fair!" Mom wiped her tears and yelled back. "I've done the best I could as a mother. I won't let you take that away from me. Who do you think gets her ready for school every day? Who do you think gives her baths, makes sure all her needs are met? It must be nice to drop by here and there to help out. Remember, it's me who makes sure that she is well taken care of every day. Me, Bill, not you!"

Dad stared at Mom for a few seconds. Layna's grip around my hand tightened.

Without saying a word, Dad began packing and taking the tents down.

"What are you doing?" Mom asked.

"We're leaving," he said. "This pretend game of being one

happy family was nice while it lasted."

That was that. The entire ride home was a silent one. Dad brought everything into the house and kissed Layna and me before leaving. He didn't even look in Mom's direction.

Mom walked up to me and said, "I'm so sorry, Lily. I should never have left you like that."

The apology just made me feel worse. She didn't need to apologize to me. This whole thing was my fault. If I weren't so helpless, none of this would have happened. I looked away because I didn't want her to see the tears of guilt in my eyes. She knew that when I turned my head away like that, I just wanted to be left alone.

Layna wheeled me to the bathroom. After helping me to the toilet, she put me in my bed, knowing I was emotionally exhausted. Unfortunately, sleep was a stubborn mule that night for both of us.

"Don't worry about them. They're stupid adults," Layna said while staring at the ceiling.

I didn't answer.

She turned toward me and asked, "Lily? Why do you think that wolf didn't hurt you?"

I mumbled a sound.

"Maybe he was really watching over you. Maybe that's why he waited until Mom got there."

Layna always had to believe the good in everything. I wasn't at all surprised at where she was going with this.

"Think about it, Lily. He could have really hurt you. You know, now that I think about it, maybe that wolf was a she. You know, a female. I mean, she could have been a mother herself so she would know to watch over her cubs. She was watching over you, Lily. I'm convinced of it! She knew you couldn't be left alone."

I suppose I could see what she was saying. The day had drained me, though, and I had no desire to think about that wolf or the fight afterward.

"I think it's so cool! I mean you were protected by a wild wolf, Lily!" The more Layna kept talking about it, the more excited she was becoming. "Do you know why that wolf protected you, Lily? It's because you're an angel—just like I told you a long time ago. You're an angel, Lily. And, that wolf knew it."

I rolled my eyes. Layna and her crazy imagination!

As far as my parents were concerned, they acted as if our vacation never occurred. Everything went back to the way it was prior to the trip. They stayed separate but cordial. Neither of them brought up the camping incident again.

But, one thing did change.

Dad hired a personal assistant to help with my needs.

Chapter Five

Although Layna continued to become more and more popular—with guys falling at her feet—she still prioritized me over anything else. Sure, she went to dances and on dates with boys, but that didn't affect our relationship at all. As a matter of fact, our bond became tighter than ever before.

During our senior year, I knew that Layna had applied to top colleges. I also knew that she was going to get into them. They would be fools not to take her since she had so much to offer. She was intelligent—scored very high on her college admission tests—and she was one of the top dancers.

As predicted, Layna was accepted into all of the colleges of her choice, and most gave her a full scholarship. The news filled my heart with joy. My sister had worked hard, and I wanted all of her dreams to come true.

Yet, a part of me tried to harden my heart because I knew that meant she would be moving away. When that day came, my fragile heart would shatter.

I decided to attend Marygrove College, which was only half an hour drive from our home in Troy, Michigan. That way, I could still live at home, and Mom or Dad could drive me to and from the college. It wasn't a big university setting. Academically, it was a great school, and I could probably pursue a degree in teaching. There was also a Master's program in Technology or Special Education, so I was going to look into both of them to see what would help me land a job after college.

As Layna and I were talking about nothing and everything one day, she suddenly brought up college. "Lily, I decided where I'm going to go to college."

Taking a deep breath, I forced myself to smile. This was not the subject I wanted to discuss.

"I'll be attending Marygrove with you. That way, I can commute from home, too."

Instantly, I held my breath, my eyes wide. Why was she saying that?

"I've weighed out all of my options, and I think this is the best for me. The college is already fully paid for with my scholarship money. And, more importantly, I get to stay home with you and Mom."

I frantically began to use my communication device. "Why? That wasn't your top choice! Are you staying here because of me?"

"No! Well, partly I am. But, mostly it's because of me!"

I couldn't help the anger that built inside me. I was so sick and tired of people changing their lives around because of me. Like I didn't already have enough guilt! Why would she do this?

I yelled at her—with my own voice.

"Why are you upset? I thought you'd be happy," Layna said, confused.

Taking a deep breath to calm myself, I steadied my head and eyes to use my device again. "You have to have your own life. I don't want you to change your goals because of me."

"I'm not, Lily. I'm still going to college. Besides, my life is with you. I told you a long time ago that I'd never leave you. Don't you remember that?"

Feeling extremely distressed, I started to drive my wheelchair away, needing some space away from her.

"Stop! We're not done talking about this!" Layna yelled behind me.

Increasing the speed of my wheelchair, I tried to dash into my room. Layna caught up to me and turned my wheelchair off.

"Sorry. I know that's mean," she said, shrugging her shoulders.

I was furious! How dare she turn off my wheelchair! She was purposefully restraining me. Weren't there laws against such abusive treatment?

I swung my arms at her, trying to land a punch. I had never lost control like that, but damn it, she couldn't ruin her life because of me. I wouldn't allow it. I continued to yell, flailing my arms, not even coming close to my target. After five minutes of screaming at her, exhaustion finally consumed me. Taking deep breaths, I bent my head down in defeat.

"Lily, please just listen to me. Remember when we were little, and that one night I had that horrible nightmare? Since that night, I've always shared your room."

I ceased my rant because suddenly I was curious. I did remember that night when we were probably around five years old. She had slept in my bedroom since that night.

When she realized that she had my attention, she said, "Well, I never told anybody about my nightmares—not even you. That night I dreamed that you were gone. I looked all over for you, but you had simply disappeared. I woke up screaming. I still have those nightmares, Lily. But, I just force my eyes open because I know I'll see you in the next bed. You see, Lily, that's why I've never left your room. I can't stand those dreams. They freak me out, but when I see you sleeping soundly, I can go back to sleep. Can you imagine if I was away for college?" Layna shuddered. "So, basically, my reasons for staying home are completely selfish. Besides, don't you know that my life is with you? How can you not know that? I'm not staying here because of you. I'm staying because of me. I don't want to be away from you."

I sighed. I didn't even know what to say.

"I can get a great education at this college, Lily. I just don't want to leave you, Mom, and Duke. I'd be miserable. I can't even picture my life without you guys. You are my everything. Please, don't make me feel bad for wanting this." Layna bit her lower lip when her voice started to shake. I know how much she hated crying in front of people—even in front of me.

Tearing up myself, I slowly brought my arm out to her. She held my hand in both of her hands and leaned toward me. "Do you understand, Lily? Do you understand how much I need you in my life?"

I nodded. Not because I understood. Not because I agreed. I nodded because that was what Layna needed at that time. And, ultimately, that was all that mattered.

Although Layna was asked to prom by the hot quarterback, James Mathis, she declined his offer. I knew she liked him, but she insisted that she had always planned on going to prom with me. When I tried to talk to her about my guilt, she dismissed my concern.

"Lily, I've always wanted to go to my senior prom with you. You know that. We've planned this for years. It's going to be amazing! How else can we make our entrance with our matching dresses?" Layna looked at me like I had lost my mind.

"James is hot. You like him," I insisted with my device. Although I wasn't surprised, a part of me was sad that no guy had asked me to the senior prom. It would have been nice if Layna and I had gone on a double date. I quickly pushed the thought away because I had learned that wishful thinking only led to more disappointments.

"He is a hottie. I agree. Don't worry, I have the whole summer to spend with him. Besides, don't forget, I've gone to so many dances without you already. You know that I've been saving this last prom dance for you. Now, I don't want to hear anything more about it. We're going to have a blast. You'll see."

I decided not to argue. She was right in a way. Layna had already attended many high school dances with her dates. She had always planned to go to the senior prom with me. A part of me knew that it was her way of making sure I attended my high school prom. I made a conscious decision not to feel guilty about it anymore. I wanted to have fun with my sister. I was going to dress up, look pretty, and dance on that dance floor.

My dress was silver and Layna's was gold. Gold always looked better on Layna because of her blonde hair. Both were sleeveless, sequin, long dresses. Layna insisted on doing my makeup and hair, and she wouldn't allow me to look in the mirror until she was done.

"Wow, Lily!" she exclaimed and finally turned my wheelchair toward the mirror.

I stared at the stranger's reflection in awe. I hardly ever wore makeup, and my hair was typically pulled up in a bun or a ponytail. While Layna beamed, I was shocked at what I saw. I actually did feel beautiful. Layna had applied just the right amount of makeup on me to enhance my green eyes and my full lips. My dark hair flowed past

31

my shoulders, the curls outlining my face.

"Say something, Lily! Do you like it?" Layna asked.

All I could do was nod. Never had I seen myself like that. As a matter of fact, I rarely even liked to look at myself in the mirror. At that moment, though, I held my head up high, unable to look away.

"I told you that you were an angel, Lily. You look just like one!" Layna kissed my cheek.

The door opened and Mom and Dad walked in. Not wanting to miss our pre-prom festivities, Dad had been there most of the day.

I heard Mom gasp, and Dad said, "My babies are all grown up. I think I need to come with you to chaperone."

"No way, Dad!" Layna shook her head, horrified at the suggestion.

"Hey, I'm just being protective of my beautiful daughters!" Dad defended himself, chuckling.

"You both truly look stunning, girls. I have to take tons of pictures." Without waiting for a response, Mom began to click away with the camera.

Attending prom with Layna would probably be one of the most memorable moments of my life. Layna had no problem driving the van with the lift so I could stay in my wheelchair. We were just too dolled up to worry about ruining our clothes while getting me in and out of the wheelchair.

Prom was held at the Hilton by the lake. As soon as we entered, I was astonished by the decorations. The fairytale theme made me feel as if I was living in my own enchanted world.

During dinner, I declined to eat. On that special night, I didn't want Layna to feed me in front of everybody. It was the one night where I wanted to feel independent and free. Layna understood instantly, so she didn't push the issue.

After dinner, Layna took me to the dance floor. Although I couldn't stand out of my wheelchair and dance without somebody supporting me, she just danced like she always did with me at home. She took my hands and moved around me while I danced from my wheelchair. At first, I was a bit self-conscious, but as soon as I saw the happiness in Layna's eyes, I relaxed. I started moving my arms and head to the beat of the music and stopped worrying about any curious eyes. This was the only prom I would ever attend, so hell, I might as well have the time of my life.

Before I knew it, a crowd of Layna's friends circled around us. They danced with us, but really they were just jumping around. They all took turns dancing with me as well—even the hot boys!

All too soon, the night was over. Everybody gave us hugs goodbyes. It felt good that Layna's friends treated me like I was one of the gang. I regretted that the fairytale night was already coming to an end.

Falling

Here and Now

Chapter Six

M y name is Lily Cooper, and I've lived with Cerebral Palsy for eighteen years. It hasn't been easy, but I've learned to make the most out of my life—at least until that dreaded ride home from prom.

Once I'm secured into the van, Layna drives toward our house. Even though it has begun to rain, it doesn't dampen my mood.

"Well?" she asks. "Wasn't that fun?"

"Ya," I answer, nodding my head. I can't remember the last time I've felt this happy.

"Did you see James? He was dancing with that red-headed bimbo all night."

"Ya," I respond. I did notice it. I'm pretty sure he was upset that Layna didn't go to prom with him and was trying to make her jealous. What an idiot!

"I guess it's good I saw his true colors. I mean, to think I would have wasted my summer on that jerk," Layna continues.

She's too good for him. I'm glad she witnessed his immature behavior.

"My summer is busy anyway. I'll be working and getting ready for college. Who has time for losers?"

Although Layna pretends like she doesn't care, I know her better. From the way she keeps talking about it and the fact that she's driving kind of fast around the curves, I can tell that James has upset her. Doesn't she realize that he has nothing on her?

"I mean, I actually saw him kissing her. He knew I was right there! He totally did that on purpose!" The more Layna continues, the more worked up she's becoming.

I desperately think of ways to try to distract her. The rain is now coming down hard, and it's becoming near impossible to see through the windshield. I bite my lip hard to swallow a scream when I feel the tires sliding on the slippery road a few times. Layna is oblivious that she's driving much too fast in the rain.

The headlights come from nowhere, blinding us. I blink, wondering why they are so bright. Where did they come from?

My heart stops beating. I hold my breath.

Layna slams on the brakes to avoid the collision.

"Hold on, Lily!" She spins the steering wheel and the van swerves out of control. I hear the screeching of the breaks and the deafening sound of the collision.

Everything moves in slow motion. Time stands still as the deathly silence encases me. I hear nothing. I feel nothing. I simply float.

And then darkness swallows me.

Beep, beep, beep, beep...

What the hell is that? Something is not right.

Beep, beep, beep, beep...

Why can't I place that sound? I have to open my eyes. For some reason, my eyelids weigh a ton.

Beep, beep, beep, beep...

Everything feels wrong. I must wake up. I must try to fix it.

Unfortunately, I'm useless. Not only do my eyes remain closed no matter how hard I try, but my unconsciousness overpowers my will to bring myself to a waking state.

Beep, beep, beep, beep...

I lose the battle and give in to the darkness once more.

"Why isn't she awake yet?" Somewhere far away in the distance, I hear Mom's voice.

"She will, honey. She's strong," Dad's quiet voice answers.

"Oh, Bill. What are we going to say to her?" Mom catches her breath.

"Shh, she may be able to hear us."

Mom's soft sobbing echoes in my ears.

"I can't stand this, Bill. Why is this happening?" Mom chokes on her words.

What's going on? Why do they sound so upset? Suddenly, the memories come flooding back. The accident. We hit something. Why can't I remember anything?

I have to open my eyes. Why isn't one of them with Layna? I have to wake up and check on her.

With all my might, I pry my eyes open. Worried sick about Layna, my arms and legs begin flailing about instantly. The more my anxiety builds, the more I lose control of my physical movements.

"Honey, honey, it's okay." I hear Dad's voice as he grabs hold of my arms.

"You're okay, Lily. Don't worry. Mommy and Daddy are right here." Mom puts her head next to mine, trying to use her "soothing" voice.

Whenever Mom uses her "soothing" voice, I know something is terribly wrong.

I yell, "Where is Layna?" Of course, the words don't come out as planned. Instead, they sound like I'm yelling and screaming in the hospital room, thrashing my body around as the beeping from the monitors go haywire.

"What's going on here?" The nurse runs into the room. "Her heart rate is going up way too high." The nurse tries to hold me down.

"She just woke up and became upset," Mom answers, now even more distressed.

"Lily, you must try to calm down." I hear Dad's stern voice attempting to settle me down.

I keep screaming, "Where is Layna?"

Nobody hears me. Nobody understands. Nobody answers.

Before I know it, the nurse injects something in my IV line, and I lose consciousness once again.

The next time I open my eyes, I force myself to remain calm. I know that's the only way I'll get any answers.

My parents are still in the room, but neither say a word about Layna. It infuriates me that they don't answer any of my questioning looks, pretending like they don't know that I'm inquiring about her.

The entire day, I try to look directly into their eyes, searching for answers. Both continue to avoid my inquiring gaze. Instead, they relentlessly fuss over me and talk about being released from the hospital soon.

"As soon as the doctor releases you, darling, you'll be coming home. It might be as early as tomorrow," Mom's soothing voice continues.

While Mom is a chatterbox, Dad remains mostly quiet. He holds my hand and watches Mom fret over me.

That night, I don't sleep a wink for fear of missing Layna in case she comes in my room. I know if there's any way she can check on me, she will find it. Nothing will stop her.

But, Layna doesn't come that night. Instead, I go home the next day with no Layna in sight.

At home, my parents keep me in bed, insisting I need to rest. Even Duke can sense that something is terribly wrong. He doesn't leave my side all day long. If it weren't for him, I would have lost my mind.

All I want is my communication device, so I can directly ask about Layna. Not only do my parents not give me the device, but they only allow me up in my wheelchair to eat and use the bathroom.

Mom continues to fuss over me. She peeks in every half an hour in my room, but doesn't say anything. While feeding me that afternoon, she insists that I have to eat. No matter how many times she puts the food in my mouth, though, it's impossible for me to swallow.

At that moment, rage builds inside me. I've never hated my parents more than I do right now. How dare they do this to me? Not giving me my communication device is the same as putting duct tape on somebody's mouth so they can't talk.

By now, the distress of not seeing Layna yet has me completely shut down. I refuse to eat, and I turn my head away every time my parents try to speak to me. The fear of the unknown eats me alive.

Later that evening, I have a complete breakdown. I scream, and I scream some more. When they try to calm me down, I scream even louder. This time, I won't stop until I get some answers.

Finally getting the message, my dad runs to my room and attaches my communication device to my wheelchair. As soon as I get my way, I stop the screaming.

"Okay, okay, Lily. You win. We need to talk," he says, sounding defeated.

Really?

I turn the device on and say, "Layna."

Mom quickly looks away and Dad clears his throat.

I say again, "Layna." This time, they will tell me where she is. She's probably wondering why I haven't tried to see her yet.

"Lily, Layna is…well, she didn't make it." Dad's voice suddenly begins to tremble.

Before I can process what he's saying, Mom continues, "She's in heaven, honey, and she's happy. But, she'll always be with us. I promise you. She'll always look after us, especially you."

What? What are they saying? How do they know that she's happy? Her family makes her happy. She should be with us.

Suddenly, it finally sinks in. Layna is dead. That's what they're saying. They're telling me she's dead.

In that instant, my world turns upside down. My heart breaks into more pieces than it's made of. The pain is so unbearable it almost feels numb. As everything crumbles around me, I fall into a deep, dark hole.

Chapter Seven

After all the years of fighting my own inner demons, nothing has ever made me feel like this. The pain cuts deep within my core, and the guilt slowly eats me alive.

It was supposed to be me. I was the one who was supposed to die in that accident. Layna should be alive. I know now that she purposefully swerved the van so that she would take most of the impact. Even until her last breath, Layna protected me.

Why? Why did she do that? Didn't she know that I'd be left torturing myself every single day, reliving that horrible drive home?

I fall and keep falling. Nothing can pull me back out.

I refuse to attend the wake and the funeral. No matter how much my parents try to persuade me, I don't budge. If I go, it will be too final. Although I know Layna is gone, I don't seem to have the courage to acknowledge it. Going to the funeral would force me to accept it.

"Lily, I know it's hard, but I think it's important to come to your sister's funeral," Dad says. "I really wish you would change your mind."

Instead of answering, I drive my wheelchair to my room and close the door.

My personal helper, Lauren, comes over before my parents leave. She enters my room and sits down on my bed. "Do you want to talk, Lily?"

I shake my head no.

"Okay, I'll leave you alone. I just want to say that I know you're really upset right now, but trust me, everything happens for a reason. You'll see. You just have to trust God."

I'll see? There is no reason for this. No reason! Layna was full of life. She was going to be somebody big. She was going to do great things in this world. She was one in a million. Why would your so-called "God" do something so cruel to somebody so special? Why would he end her life when she had just begun to live? There is no reason. And no, I will never see.

Because I want to be left alone, I scream at her. I don't stop screaming until she says, "Fine, I'm leaving. I'll be outside your room if you need anything."

Later, I find out that everybody from school came to Layna's funeral. Why wouldn't they? She was loved by so many. Everybody said goodbye to her. Everybody, except for me.

That day, as Layna is buried underground, I bury myself into my personal hell hole.

Maybe pain is its own entity. Maybe that's why it has the power to consume one's soul.

I refuse to attend the graduation. I can't even imagine being there without Layna. Most days, I stay in my room with Duke. Even when my high school diploma is mailed to me, I don't have any interest in opening it.

The next two years are the worst two years of my life. Although Dad has permanently moved in, I have completely shut down. My mom is not doing much better. Dad has both of us in therapy, and we're both on anti-depressants. They don't help. Some days it hurts so bad that I just want to end it all. Maybe I'll find Layna in the afterlife.

So, I die slowly every day. I can't let the past go. I can't say goodbye to Layna. I can't cry. I can't smile. I can't eat. I just exist.

Duke is the only one who motivates me to wake up every morning. He has become my best friend. I swear he can sense my every emotion. Maybe Layna was right about animals. Maybe they do have a sixth sense. Maybe that's the reason I don't need to talk for him to understand my feelings.

Although I have no will to leave the house, Dad forces me to go to college. He comes into my room one day and says, "You can't lock yourself in your room forever, Lily. It doesn't work that way. You may hate me for this, but since you're in no state to make any decisions, I'm going to make them for you. You will go to college and get your degree. You have no choice in that matter."

And that's that. I know my father enough to know that when he puts his foot down on something, that's the end of the discussion.

I schedule my classes so they're either lumped together before lunch on a particular day or after lunch. That way, I don't have to worry about eating lunch there. Luckily, Dad's job is flexible enough where he can take me and pick me up.

I force myself to go through the motions. Not because I agree. I do it for him. After all, Dad has to be strong not only for me, but also for Mom.

I soon learn that college keeps me busy. The busier I remain, the more the pain stays away. Some days are actually somewhat tolerable.

When Dad brings me home from college one day, I sense immediately that something is wrong with Duke. He normally greets me at the door, but today, he has remained in this doggy bed.

I immediately drive my wheelchair to him, and he slowly lifts his head at me.

Dad follows me and sits next to Duke. "What's wrong, boy?"

He then brings him some food and water, but Duke refuses both. Dad tries to stand him up, but after a couple of steps, Duke collapses.

"Let's take him to the vet, Lily, and ask the doctor what's wrong with our boy." He calls Mom at work and notifies her.

My head spins the entire ride to the vet. Feeling nauseated from worrying, I wait anxiously until the vet can speak to us. We find out that Duke seems to be having mini strokes. He says sometimes they stop on their own, but occasionally they can lead to a major stroke.

"Duke is old now, and sometimes this happens. Really, unless you're willing to spend a lot of money on tests and surgeries, I don't know what else you can do. Because of his age, I don't even recommend any surgeries. He probably wouldn't survive it."

I hold back the tears until I reach home. Once Dad puts Duke on his bed, I request to lie down with him. Dad places me next to Duke, and I hug him tight.

When Mom rushes home from work, she lies down with us as well, right there on the floor. "I'm so sorry, Lily." Hearing Mom's shaky voice and seeing her red eyes, I know she's been crying as well.

The rest of the evening, I refuse to do anything else but stay with Duke. Finally, as the night progresses, Dad carries both of us to my bed.

As I continue to cuddle with Duke all night, I think of all of our happy moments. I wonder if he can sense thoughts because once in a while he kisses my face or my hand.

Duke, you are my everything. I wish you would stay with me. Besides Layna, you've been the only one who has understood me. What am I going to do without you?

Duke once again kisses me.

I hope you're not in any pain. God, please don't let him hurt. If he's coming to you, please help him find Layna.

Through the tears, the thought of Layna and Duke being together gives me some sense of peace.

As Duke's breathing becomes shallower, I can't seem to stop my sobbing. Mom and Dad must have heard me because they run into my room. They both kneel around the bed, knowing the end is near.

Duke, I love you and always will. Thank you for being my best friend.

Somehow, Duke manages to open his eyes. He looks straight at me and kisses my tears. Just as quickly, his eyes close, and I can barely hear him breathing. Desperately, I try to give him one more message.

Duke, look for Layna. She will be waiting for you. Please tell her I'll see her soon.

He is gone.

And "soon" doesn't come soon enough for me.

My depression goes from bad to worse. I continue to attend college, but I stay to myself. My parents can't help me. The medicines can't help me. And, my psychiatrist can't help me.

I have no idea of the purpose of my existence anymore. I question what it is in this world that is still keeping me alive.

If nothing else, at least my parents seem to have picked up the pieces and have found one another again. It gives me a sense of peace to see them happy. I know that Layna would have been ecstatic to see them together like this.

As I watch their interaction during dinner, I wonder about human nature. It has taken Layna's death for them to realize their love for one another. I sigh. People take so much for granted. If they only realize how lucky they are before it's too late. I guess losing something so precious has opened my parents' eyes to what's been right in front of them all along.

Letting Go

Living Again

Chapter Eight

I'm alive. I'm breathing, eating, using the bathroom, attending the college courses to get my degree, and I'm functioning day by day. Yes, I'm alive. But, am I living?

As I wait anxiously for Dad to pick me up from college, I watch the storm worsening. I can't help but worry about my dad driving on the slippery roads. Every time it rains or snows, my heart instantly beats faster as my anxiety increases.

Dad is later than usual. Squinting my eyes, I try to see through the large snowflakes. It looks like a blizzard outside. Because it's the last day before winter break begins, I've purposely made the effort to make it to classes, not wanting to miss anything. Watching the storm, I already regret my decision.

Dad always pulls the van right by the curb. Since I wait for him in the cafeteria with large glass windows that face the parking lot, I have a perfect view when he pulls up. Normally, he likes to come into the building to bring me to the van.

From my calculation, he's running about half an hour late. I suppose I shouldn't worry. With the bad roads, this is to be expected. I try to take some deep breaths to calm my nerves.

Please let him be okay. Please let him be okay. Please let him be okay.

"Hi, do you need help?"

I swing my head toward the voice and notice hazel eyes staring at me. Instantly, I take in the stranger's good looks. He appears to be in his mid-twenties with wavy, brown hair, almost down to his shoulders. He seems carefree and even a bit wild, as I notice the disheveled hair and tiny hoops on both ears. As a slight smile plays on his lips, I'm suddenly embarrassed for staring at him. Remembering that he's still waiting for my answer, I shake my head no. As his intense eyes continue to bore into me, I quickly look away. Why is he here? Nobody talks to me. Ever.

"Are you sure?" he insists.

"I'm fine," I answer with my device.

"Huh, okay. Well, you don't mind if I hang out with you for a while, do you? You know, just until your ride gets here." Without waiting for an answer, he pulls a chair up next to me.

Feeling annoyed, I just want him to leave me alone so I can focus on my dad. I turn my attention to stare out of the window, trying very hard to ignore him.

"Lily, right? Your name is Lily?"

What the hell? How does he know that? Maybe if I continue to disregard him, he'll think I don't understand him and leave. I've learned this trick through the years, and it always works.

"I'm Chance." Apparently, the trick doesn't work with him.

Not turning to acknowledge him, my attention stays on what's happening outside, praying I would see the headlights of the van soon.

"I've seen you around. You know, driving around here. I've been meaning to talk to you for a while now, but just didn't have the guts to do it. When I saw you still waiting for your ride, I jumped at the opportunity." Chance chuckles under his breath.

I am more confused than ever. Why is he talking to me? What does he want? Should I be worried? There's really nobody else around, except for the people who occasionally walk out of the door. Is this guy some kind of a creep who can hurt me? He doesn't look like a creep, though. Actually, he's absolutely gorgeous. He's tall, muscular build, with hazel eyes surrounded by thick, dark eyelashes, and a smile that can melt one's heart. But, I don't dare look his way.

"Are you going to continue ignoring me?" he asks, leaning closer to me.

Wow! He really doesn't know how to take the hint. Finally, I turn to him and with my device, I say, "What do you want?"

As his smile widens, Chance's eyes tease me. "I was wondering when I was going to get on your nerves."

"What do you want?" I repeat.

"Just wanna talk."

Without responding, I stare out the window again.

"Okay, guess you don't want to talk. That's cool. I'm still not leaving until your ride gets here. I don't really feel like driving in that mess right now anyway."

I decide that maybe he's worried about me sitting here by myself. He probably feels sorry for me.

"So what's your story?" he asks.

I glance toward him, and my heart instantly skips a beat when I notice his arched eyebrows and his lopsided grin.

"What?" I ask, not sure what he means.

"I mean, I've been noticing this beautiful girl with long, dark hair and those killer green eyes for a while now. But, I've never seen her gorgeous eyes smile. I can't help but wonder what her story is. You got any ideas?" His voice softens.

Caught off guard, my eyes fill with unshed tears. Damn it! I don't want to fall apart in front of this complete stranger. I quickly turn my head away, attempting to hide my distress.

"Hey, I'm sorry, Lily. I didn't mean to upset you. Man, I suck with first impressions." Chance reaches to touch my hand.

Startled, I snatch mine away.

"Lily, Lily! Sorry I'm so late." I recognize Dad's voice. As he rushes toward me, he glares at Chance suspiciously. Placing a reassuring hand on my shoulder, he asks, "You okay?"

I nod.

"Hello, sir. I was just keeping Lily company until her ride arrived." Chance stands up and extends his hand.

Shaking his hand, Dad says, "Oh, I see. Thank you. I appreciate that. I'm Bill Cooper, Lily's father. And you are?"

"Chance. Chance Ryker. I'm taking some classes here."

"I see. Okay, well, nice to meet you, Chance. We have to head out now. Roads are bad out there so drive carefully." Dad nods his head at Chance. He turns to me and says, "You ready, Lily? Sorry I didn't text you, but I didn't want to do that while I was driving."

I nod my head and start driving my wheelchair toward the door.

"It was nice talking to you, Lily. Oh, and Merry Christmas," Chance yells behind me.

Ignoring him, I drive away from this stranger who somehow has gotten under my skin.

When I return to school after the break, thoughts of Chance linger in my mind. No matter how hard I have tried to not think about him, I have failed miserably.

As I drive to my classes, I review my new schedule in my mind. I'm in my second semester of my junior year already, so I've become very familiar with this college. So far, I've done very well in my classes because I have buried myself in my schoolwork since college started.

My thoughts drift back to Chance. I wonder why he took the time to talk to me that day. The idea of him communicating with me because he felt sorry for me makes me cringe.

I purposefully push him out of my mind. I need to focus on my new schedule since I have three classes back to back today. The good news is that I should be done by twelve, so I'll be home all afternoon. I plan on using that time to become familiar with the new material from my classes.

After finishing the first two classes, I release a sigh of relief. The teachers are nice, and although I notice some curious looks thrown at me, it's nothing unusual for me. Just one more class to go and my day will be done. It should be fairly easy since it's the Ethics class.

I arrive before class starts. This is my normal practice since I like to get there before other students and find an inconspicuous spot in the corner. This one is mostly a lecture, so it's held in the auditorium.

Realizing that I am the first one there, I quickly position myself in the far corner of the room, away from the door. Now, most people shouldn't notice me unless they're seated by me. I prepare my communication device to record the lecture. This particular feature on the device has been a lifesaver for me.

Soon, the class fills and the professor enters.

"Good morning, class. I'm Professor Locklear. This is a fast-moving class so be ready. We will mostly have lectures in here. However, there will occasionally be some discussions. I have a Teacher's Assistant, who will be helping me out during these discussions. Please welcome Chance Ryker."

My head flings up at the mention of his name. To my utter shock, Chance's tall, lean frame walks in, and he takes his place in the front while Professor Locklear begins his lecture.

What the hell! I nearly choke on my saliva. Not wanting to start coughing, I swallow hard and try to calm down. He teaches here? I thought he said he was taking classes at this college. Confused, I try to sink further into my wheelchair. I don't want him to notice me.

As my nervousness increases, so does my inability to control my muscles. I have to use all of my energy to calm my muscles down. I try to focus on what the professor is saying, but it's useless. All I see is Chance from my peripheral vision.

Instead of paying attention to the lecture, I weigh my options on how I can leave undetected. My best bet may be to try to leave in the middle of the crowd. Normally, I wait until the entire class leaves before exiting. This time, though, I'm going to just speed out of here as soon as I can when everybody else exits. Hopefully, I can hide among the rest of the students.

Unfortunately, I know that if he doesn't notice me today, he will on another day. Why wouldn't he? After all, I'm the only person in here in a wheelchair who can't talk on my own.

With my heartbeat completely out of control, I decide that my best option is to drop this class. Yes, that's what I'll do. I'll just take it next year.

What the hell is wrong with me? I'm going to allow some guy I don't even know chase me out of this class? He probably doesn't even remember me. Trying to understand why I'm acting so irrationally, I close my eyes and count to ten.

I finally figure it out. I don't like the way he makes me feel. He is a complete stranger, and yet, he has been on my mind day and night since I've met him. Okay, I need to get a grip here. I need the rational Lily back.

As soon as the class is over, I drive my wheelchair right in the middle of the crowd and race out of there. I don't dare look anywhere but my driving path. Hopefully, he doesn't notice me. I must have been holding my breath because as soon as I'm down the hall, I release a long sigh of relief.

Just when I think that I'm home free, I hear the familiar voice behind me—the voice that has haunted my dreams at night for the last couple of weeks.

"Lily, wait up!"

Damn, damn, damn! I keep driving, hoping he'll think I didn't hear him. My efforts are to no avail, though, because he soon catches up with me.

"Hey, Lily!" he exclaims as he keeps his pace with my wheelchair. "It's Chance. We met right before the break. I wasn't sure if you remembered me."

What? Who the hell would forget such a beautiful man? I barely acknowledge him and keep driving my wheelchair.

"Well, the way you're ignoring me, I guess you do remember me. I want to talk to you for a minute. Where are you going right now? Do you have a break?" Apparently, Chance doesn't give up easily.

I'm done with my day, so I continue driving toward the cafeteria. Dad should be picking me up from there during his lunch break. Chance must really want to say something because he follows me to the cafeteria. Once I find my place in my usual spot, he pulls the chair next to me.

I sigh. Okay, I can continue to ignore him or just find out what he wants. He obviously is not planning on leaving anytime soon.

"What do you want?" I ask with my device.

"Just wanna catch up. How was your Christmas?"

How was my Christmas? It sucked! Every holiday has sucked since Layna's death. I purposefully don't answer him.

"Okay, fine, we don't want to small talk. I'll be straight up with you. I want to get to know you better, Lily. You seem like a cool girl and well…maybe we can try to be friends?"

I finally face him. Still suspicious, I use my device. "Why?"

"Why not?" Chance raises one eyebrow as a tiny smirk plays at the corner of his mouth.

I sigh. This is useless. "You're a teacher here, not a student. Why did you say you were a student?"

"I *am* taking classes here. I'm also a teacher's assistant for a couple of the classes. I only attend school part time here. Actually, I work full time as a nurse, but want to get more classes under my belt before applying to medical schools. So, that's what I'm doing here."

He's a nurse? And he wants to be a physician. Well, now it all makes sense. No wonder he's drawn to me. He probably sees me as one of his patients.

"Look, don't treat me like one of your patients, okay?" I blurt out. Luckily, I've gotten pretty fast at using my communication device, so there's not too much of a delay when I respond.

At first his eyes widen in surprise. Then, he laughs—an outright, full-blown laughter. He must have laughed for full fifteen seconds. This may not seem long, but as I sit there staring at him in disbelief, those fifteen seconds seem like an eternity.

When he finally is able to contain himself, he says, "Trust me, Lily. I definitely do not see you as one of my patients since I work in a nursing home, and the average age is over eighty."

"Do you have a hero complex or something?"

Chance laughs again. "What? Isn't that like somebody who deliberately does bad things like setting fires and then tries to act like the hero?"

I roll my eyes.

"Do I need to have a specific reason to talk to a pretty girl?" he asks.

I narrow my eyes at him, still suspicious of his intent. "Are you trying to flirt?"

"I'm not trying to flirt. I *am* flirting." Chance throws me his lopsided grin.

"You're my teacher. Teachers are not supposed to flirt with their students. Aren't there rules against that?" In those short moments, he has put me at ease, and my feisty personality surfaces.

"Well, technically I'm not your teacher. I'm just a teacher's assistant. I'm sure that's different."

"You're sure, huh?"

"Yep, pretty sure. Are you done for the day?"

"Yes. My dad will be here soon to get me."

"I see. I'm back again on Wednesday for that class. Can we meet after class? Maybe we can do lunch together."

Lunch? Does he not realize I can't feed myself? I quickly look away.

Immediately sensing his mistake, Chance says, "Err, okay, I screwed that one up. We can just talk after class here until your ride comes. I don't mind that."

"Why? What do you want to talk about?"

"We're back to the same question again? I told you, you've caught my attention. To be honest, I've been watching you for a while now. I think they call people like me stalkers. Don't say I never warned you."

That makes me laugh.

"Finally! You need to do that more often," Chance says, his hazel eyes turning darker.

I look at him in confusion.

"Laugh. I love hearing you laugh. Remember to laugh more." I look away. He's right, of course. I can't remember laughing like that since Layna's been gone.

"Shit. Looks like I hit a nerve. I'm sorry, Lily. Do you want to talk about it?" Chance reaches to hold my hand.

This time, I don't pull away. This time, I enjoy the human touch. I slowly shake my head no, not willing to open any wounds.

Chance stares out of the window with me, but he keeps his hand on mine. Suddenly embarrassed by the intimate touch, I slide my hand away. The only people who have hugged, kissed, or held my hands have been my parents and Layna.

I think he must have forgotten that he was holding my hand because he, too, briefly looks embarrassed. His teasing smirk quickly returns, though, and he says, "There's your dad. We'll talk again on Wednesday. I don't want him to find me with you again, or he really will think I'm some kind of a crazy stalker."

I flash him a quick smile, and he soon disappears down the hall with his long strides.

Chapter Nine

For the next few months, Chance and I talk after class every Monday and Wednesday. The conversations remain light, but soon we both begin to feel comfortable with one another. I see Chance not only for his good looks, but I soon appreciate him for his intelligence. Chance has a gift of making people feel at ease, and every day, he has me laughing at his sarcastic sense of humor. Sometimes, I even tell my dad to pick me up a bit later so I can spend more time with Chance.

He calls me beautiful often in our conversations. I convince myself that he's just a nice guy and probably says that to make me feel good. It's not that nobody has ever called me beautiful before. I've heard it from my parents, Layna, therapists, and even my teachers. Aren't they supposed to say that, though? I mean, my parents are always going to think I'm beautiful. I'm their child for God's sake. As far as the teachers and therapists go, I'm sure they are trained to help students' self-esteems. The teachers probably tell all their students that, especially the ones with special needs.

But one night, I drive my wheelchair to the mirror in my room and stare at my reflection. I've never paid too much attention to my looks. Usually, my mom or my personal helpers pull my hair up in a ponytail or a bun. I never wear makeup unless it's for a special occasion. As I look in the mirror, for the first time in my life, I actually see a pretty girl staring back at me. I notice my large, almond-shaped, emerald green eyes, surrounded by long, black eyelashes. My porcelain skin is a sharp contrast against my dark hair. I must have gotten the dark hair from my mother's Italian side, while Layna had the blonde hair from Dad's Swedish side.

I touch my face and smile.

For the first time, I realize that I *am* pretty.

For the first time in my life, I don't notice that I'm in a wheelchair.

Over the weekend, my parents and I head to the mall to shop. I'm looking forward to buying some new clothes. Normally, I don't even enjoy shopping. My mom usually buys my clothes since I've never really cared about what I wear. This time, though, I want to pick out my own outfits and look nice, especially at the college.

After shopping for a few hours—content with my new wardrobe—we start heading out. To my surprise, just as we're about to exit the mall, Chance walks in. Shocked, I almost run my wheelchair into the wall. I force myself to settle myself down and avoid making an utter fool out of myself.

He notices me instantly and smiles. As he approaches us, I notice a tall woman, who appears to be in her twenties, walking alongside him. My mouth drops open when I notice her gorgeous looks. She has long auburn hair, blue eyes, and she's very confident as she strides toward us. Chance must be over six feet and she's at least 5 feet 8 inches. With her heels on, she looks like a model next to him. To be honest, they look like a Hollywood couple.

"Lily, hey! Fancy seeing you here," Chance says when he reaches us.

I continue to stare, dumbfounded, with my mouth still open in shock.

"Oh, hi there! Chance, right?" Dad saves the day by intervening and allowing me some time to compose myself. "Honey, this is Chance, Lily's friend."

"Oh, yes. Hi, Chance. It's so nice to meet you," Mom says, sounding overly cheerful. She can tell that not only am I shocked, but also distressed.

"Chance, are you going to introduce us?" asks the woman I already hate. How can anybody look so perfect?

"Err, yeah. Sorry about that. This is Beca. And Beca, this is Lily and her parents." Chance moves next to me.

"Oh, of course! This is your special friend from college. I've heard such great things about you, Lily." Beca leans toward me, talking slowly and loudly, as if I can't understand what she's saying.

It's official. I hate her. She's patronizing me and treating me like a child. I don't know which is worse.

With my device, I answer, "Actually, there's nothing special about me. I'm just Lily. Oh, and by the way, just because I have Cerebral Palsy doesn't mean I'm deaf and can't understand you. You don't have to talk loud." I simply can't resist.

While Mom looks mortified, Chance chuckles under his breath and Dad tries to hide his smile.

"Oh, of course, Lily. I didn't mean…" As Beca keeps talking, I turn my wheelchair toward the door and exit out. It may have been rude, but I have no desire to listen to her condescending tone any longer. Yes, I've been used to it my entire life, but I'm done putting up with ignorant people.

Once in the van, Mom asks, "Wow, Lily. What was that about?"

"Don't want to talk about it," I abruptly answer.

"Hey, I'm glad you put her back in her place. She looked like a total ditz to me," Dad chimes in.

I know he's trying to make me feel better, but it doesn't help. As much as I fight thinking about it, I fail miserably. Chance has never mentioned that he has a girlfriend. Well, why would he need to mention that to me? I mean, he's just intrigued by me. That doesn't mean he doesn't have a life. Just because all I do is go to school and come home, with no social life at all, doesn't mean his is the same. As a matter of fact, with his charismatic personality, I'm sure he has a very active social lifestyle.

Maybe she's not his girlfriend, but I push the thought away quickly. She seemed too familiar with him, and he has obviously talked about me to her. How dare he say anything about me to his girlfriend?

As soon as we arrive home, I rush to my room. I want to be left alone. This is all my fault. I've allowed myself to dream. Haven't I learned by now that dreaming will only lead to disappointments?

For the rest of the weekend, I mostly stay to myself. I don't want to go to class next week. I'm just not ready to see him. How can I possibly explain my irrational behavior to him? And knowing him, he will confront me about it.

On Monday, I decide I'm too sick to go to my classes and will get the online notes. I have no desire to see Chance. As a matter of fact, I need to start distancing myself from him. That's the only way I'll be able to protect myself from getting hurt.

My personal helper, Lauren, comes to help me during the day. Although I stay in bed most of the morning, Lauren eventually forces me to take a shower and come out of my room for lunch. After eating, I hide myself back in my room.

Since Layna's passing, I listen to *The Lonely* by Christina Perri quite a bit. Layna used to love dancing to *Perfect* with me, but I refuse to play that song since Layna's been gone. Instead, I lose myself in the lyrics of *The Lonely*. When I'm feeling down, that song is perfect for me. I like to lock myself in my room and blast that song. Today is one of those days.

I play the song on repeat, torturing myself with every line— every word.

I don't even hear the knock on my door when Lauren walks in. "Lily, you have a visitor."

Confused, I turn to see who the hell would visit me. I almost fall out of my wheelchair when I see Chance stroll in behind Lauren. My eyes must have bulged out of my sockets because Chance can't hide his smirk.

"Seems like you guys know each other. I'll be in the kitchen if you need anything, Lily." Lauren turns to leave. Before she closes the door, she points to Chance and mouths, "Hot!" Luckily, his back is still to her, so he doesn't notice the exchange.

"Surprised to see me?" Chance asks.

Surprised? That's putting it mildly!

"How did you know where I live? What are you doing here?" I fire off the questions with my device.

"Being a teacher's assistant does have some perks. For example, I already have all of the students' names, numbers, and addresses. When I didn't see you in class, I was worried. So, I wanted to check on you."

"I don't need you to check on me. I'm fine!" I'm really starting to believe that he thinks of me as some sort of a subject on whatever experiment he's doing. A part of me is happy to see him, but another part of me is infuriated that he's checking up on me like I'm a child.

"I can see you're fine! Why didn't you come to class, then?"

"Not your business!" Damn, I wish I can make this device yell at him. I'm pretty sure, though, that he can see from the expression on my face how angry I'm becoming. Just then, the song ends and starts again.

"And, why do you have this song on repeat? Wow, talk about a depressing song!" Chance walks toward me.

"What do you want?" I finally ask. Clearly, he's not planning on leaving.

Chance waits a few seconds, contemplating. He sets his lips in a thin line and says, "Dance with me."

"What?"

"Dance with me, Lily. And, we're going to dance to this song."

"No!"

"No?"

"No!" I repeat. What is wrong with this guy?

Chance ignores me and removes my leg rests out of the way. "Would you do me the honor of dancing with me, Miss Cooper?"

"No," I yell, this time with my own voice. It may not have been the perfect "no," but he hears me loud and clear.

He laughs under his breath and says, "You are adorable when you're mad."

Does he think this is a joke? Without saying anything further, Chance takes my seat belt off and stands me up. He must realize that I can't support my full weight on my legs because he has a good hold around my torso. Once my feet touch the floor, he brings me into his embrace and sways to the music. Even though at first I feel uneasy, I eventually allow myself to relax. This actually feels really good. I've never been held this close by anybody but my family.

I rest my head on his chest as the haunting lyrics fill the room. Chance holds me tighter, and I feel his strength and power spread through me. He makes me feel secure…protected. I feel his fingers run through my hair as his soft caresses send shivers down my spine. I sigh, knowing I'm setting myself up for heartbreak.

Once the song finishes, Chance assists me to sit back down in my wheelchair. After securing me, he sets up the communication device so I can access it.

"That wasn't so bad, was it? Now, every time you listen to this depressing song, hopefully, you'll have some happy memories associated with it." Chance sits back down on my bed.

I can't help but smile because I do feel much better.

"Now, that's what I like to see. So, tell me whose pictures are all over your room." Chance picks up Layna's photo from my bedside table.

He's right. My room is covered with Layna's pictures, and her empty bed still sits on the other side. I've refused to allow my parents to move any of her things out of my room. It's been three years since she's been gone, but I'm still not ready to let her go.

"My sister," I reply.

Chance looks at me and frowns. "I didn't know you had a sister. For some reason, I thought you were an only child."

"She died," I simply say.

"Oh, man. I'm sorry, Lily. Do you want to talk about it?"

I abruptly shake my head no.

"Ok, fair enough. Listen, I also stopped by because I'm embarrassed by my friend's behavior the other day. Beca can be clueless at times. She's just wrapped up in her own world. I was waiting all weekend to talk to you. When you didn't show up to class, I couldn't wait any longer to get it off of my chest. So I decided to head over here. I've been feeling bad about it."

"Why are you dating such a clueless person?" I know it's not my business, but he's the one who called her clueless.

"I'm not dating her," Chance says, surprised.

I remain silent but look away.

"She's my friend, Lily. If you must know, then yes, we did date a long time ago. We were in high school, but we grew apart. We're completely different people now. Beca was in town, so we hung out on Saturday. That's it. She's definitely not my girlfriend nor do I have any feelings toward her like that."

A part of me is relieved, but the more cautious part—the one that keeps the invisible walls up—wonders if he's telling the truth. What can I say about it, though? I have no right to ask any more questions about the matter, nor do I have the right to feel jealous.

After I remain silent, Chance says, "Can I ask you a question?"

I glance toward him, now curious.

"When we danced, you were able to put weight on your legs and move. Are you able to walk with help? You don't have to answer if you don't want to."

"I walked better when I was younger. I can still walk with help, but very short distances."

"Do you practice walking often so your muscles don't get weaker?"

"You said one question." But I smile. I consider Chance my friend, so I don't mind talking to him. I've never had a friend who has cared enough to ask.

"True, I did say that, but I lied." Chance smirks, lifting one eyebrow.

"I've had physical therapy my entire life. Once insurance stopped paying for it, my parents had to pay out of pocket, which can get very expensive. During the week, I still receive therapy once a week. On weekends, I attend an aqua therapy class as well. That's my favorite because I can do so much more in the water." Just remembering how relaxed my muscles feel during those sessions makes me smile.

"Yeah? Maybe I can go with you sometime."

"No, the sessions are long and you would be bored."

"Can't I go in the pool with you?"

"Well…they do allow family and friends to participate—more for training purposes. But I don't know."

"Let me go with you this weekend, Lily. I'm curious, that's all. Besides, I'd love to see how you move in the water." Chance winks, teasing me.

"You're crazy. But okay, fine. Don't complain if you get bored. I tried to warn you."

"You got yourself a deal. I gotta go to work soon. I'll e-mail you the notes from class today. You get all the e-mails on that device of yours?"

"Yeah, I have all internet access with this thing. It's been a lifesaver." I say, placing my hand on my device.

Chance remains silent, lost in his thoughts. The teasing Chance is gone, replaced by the more serious one.

"It's all good, Chance. I'm used to it," I interrupt his thoughts.

As if coming back to reality, he smiles. "Yes, I see you're all good. Well, thank you, mademoiselle, for the wonderful dance. Be looking out for my email tonight, and I'll see you Wednesday in class." Chance bows dramatically in front of me and strolls out of my room.

Later that night, I receive an e-mail from him that says, "Hey, beautiful, here are the notes from class (see attachment). Remember, no more dancing in an empty room. Sweet dreams, Lily."

"Good night, Chance," I reply back.

Sometimes, life can seem very bleak. But, if you wait long enough and look hard enough, you may see a glimmer of light through the darkness…bringing with it, a hint of hope. And, that

tiny sliver of hope may just save your soul.
That night, I fall asleep smiling.

Chapter Ten

When I tell my parents that Chance will be attending the aqua therapy session on Saturday, neither responds to the news. I wait for the questions, the lectures, the disapprovals, but instead, they simply nod and walk away. This suits me just fine because I have no desire to discuss Chance with them.

True to his word, Chance joins me in the pool. I feel a bit uncomfortable in the beginning because I'm in my swimsuit, and I have to be wheeled down the ramp with the pool chair. Chance doesn't seem to think anything strange about it. As a matter of fact, he brings the chair into the water and lifts me out. It's amazing the thoughts that run through one's mind when placed in a vulnerable situation like this.

Damn, his body is hotter than I had imagined.

Thank you, Mom, for always being obsessive about shaving my legs and all of my personal areas.

Thank God I've always had a fit body.

Hope my swimsuit is on correctly and nothing is sticking out.

Hope my body behaves for once in my life. Please don't let me hit him on the head accidently!

Taking a deep breath, I force myself to relax so the water can do its magic.

Chance is a good listener because he follows all the directions from the therapist. She shows him how to help me walk, and how to facilitate as well as stretch my muscles. Since he's a nurse, he picks up the techniques with ease.

It feels good to have Chance work with me in the water. I feel so much more in control of my body in here. I'm also pretty good at walking in the pool if I have some assistance. I show him everything I can do, including swimming on my back with a neck collar.

"Let's try this, Lily," Trina, my therapist, says and brings me to a corner to work on standing squats while holding the rail. Making sure Chance is out of earshot, she whispers, "He's so hot, Lily. Where did you find him?"

I laugh because Trina has been my therapist forever. I would even consider her my friend because I know she genuinely cares for me. I smile smugly, excited to have Chance in my life.

"What are you guys working on?" Chance sneaks up on us, standing on the other side of me.

"We're doing squats now. Do you want to work with Lily while I go help my other patients?" Trina asks.

"Absolutely," Chance answers. After Trina swims away, Chance asks, "What was she whispering to you?"

My smile widens, throwing him a mischievous look.

"Girl talk, eh? Holding secrets from me, eh? Well, that calls for payback."

Before I can react, Chance grabs me by the waist and turns me around to face him. As he holds me in his embrace, he wraps my legs around his waist. Before I can resist, he takes me for a spin. He twirls me around and purposefully splashes water on me. With my arms and legs wrapped around him as I hold on for dear life, all I can do is laugh. Even the therapists and the other patients cheer for Chance.

Before long, all of the patients gather around us, and Chance quickly has them under his spell. He compliments everybody on how well they're doing and encourages them to continue working hard. He is certainly gifted with that charismatic personality that draws people to him.

As our friendship becomes stronger, Chance and I spend more time together. He attends my therapy sessions when he's available and comes over at least a couple of times a week. We even pick our classes for the following year according to when we can meet up at school. I'm excited that it will be my last year before I graduate. I'm ready to be out there working and bringing home a real paycheck.

During the summer break, Chance and I grow very close. I finally learn to let my walls down and trust him. As my comfort level increases around him, I don't worry too much about my disabilities. We talk about everything and nothing. Sometimes, we argue about politics, TV shows, favorite movies, and favorite books. Chance has somehow slipped into my life and has become my best friend.

He usually comes over or takes me to the movies, and on most days, we usually go on our evening strolls. Our strolls consist of Chance walking next to me while I drive my wheelchair.

During our walk one evening, I ask him about his family. He has yet to mention anything about his personal life.

"I don't really have any family, Lily. I was an only child, and my parents died a few years ago."

"Oh, sorry." I stop my wheelchair because I want to talk to him properly.

"It's cool. It was a while ago." Although he says this, I can tell the conversation is making him uncomfortable.

"What about uncles and aunts? Other family?"

"My family is from Colorado. I was never very close to my extended family. Once my parents died, I moved away. I suppose I could have tried to keep in touch with everybody, but I just needed to get away from it all. I moved here to Michigan and got a job as a nurse. Now, I consider this my home."

"So you're all alone here?" I ask as a wave of sadness washes over me.

"Well, no! I've made a lot of friends here, and I've got you! Of course, I'm not alone." Chance winks, teasing me.

Although I smile, I know he's using one of his tactics to change the subject.

"Can you do me a favor? Can you take me to Layna's gravesite?" I ask.

Chance looks surprised, but says, "Of course, Lily."

"I need to do something I should have done a long time ago."

Usually, when Chance and I go out, we use my parents' van since it is wheelchair accessible. He never lets me sit in the wheelchair in the back, though. He says my place is in the front, next to him.

When we return to the house from our stroll, Chance takes the van keys and lifts me to the passenger seat. He places the belt on me and parks the wheelchair in the back. He has already taken the directions from my parents, so he knows where to go.

Lost in my thoughts, I can't help but be nervous about going to visit Layna. I've never gone there, even when my parents have asked me to go with them. I know I've avoided it long enough, and it's time to face my fears. With Chance by my side, I can tackle anything.

They say fear may prompt one of two responses: forget everything and run or face everything and rise. I've been hiding all this time—running from my fears. It's time to accept what happened. It's time to let Layna go.

When we reach the cemetery, Chance is easily able to find Layna's site with my parents' directions. Luckily, we're able to drive my wheelchair all the way to her gravestone.

Once there, my anxiety increases. Maybe this is not the right time. Maybe I'm not ready for this. Seeing her name engraved on the stone brings back all of the memories. I can't say goodbye—not yet.

Sensing my panic, Chance places his hand on mine. "It'll be okay, Lily. I'll help you."

I focus on him, allowing his strength to help me find my courage.

"Do you want me to bring you down to the ground?" he asks, squeezing my hand.

I nod, needing to be close to Layna.

Chance carries me out of the wheelchair and lowers me down by her stone. He sits behind me so I can lean against him. I take a deep breath and read the words.

In Loving Memories of
Layna Grace Cooper
Beloved Daughter, Cherished Sister
Heart of Gold, Never Forgotten

A sob escapes me as tremors crawl through my body.

Oh, Layna, I am so sorry. I should have come sooner. I just couldn't do it. You were always the brave one between us. God, how I've missed you. These years without you have been so hard. I hope you're doing well. I hope you're happy. I know I should have come to the funeral. It was the right thing to do. I should have stood by Mom and Dad and helped bury you. I should have, Layna. I just couldn't. I wasn't ready to let you go yet.

The tears continue to flow. By now, I'm sobbing out loud. Instantly, Chance holds me tighter in his embrace. He doesn't say anything. He doesn't disturb me. He simply holds me, silently providing me his strength.

I wanted to check on you today. I wanted you to see that I'm doing better. I'm slowly getting my life together. Hell, I'll be graduating from college next year, Layna! Can you believe that? I'm all grown up now, Layna. How I wish you were with me. We'd be graduating together.

I pause, trying to control my emotions.

Layna, why did you have to leave? I was angry with you for the longest time. I blamed you for turning your steering wheel the way you did. You could have been here today, Layna, if you didn't do that.

The pain in my heart is unbearable. I turn my face into Chance's chest and holler in pain. It doesn't matter that I'm screaming. It doesn't matter that his shirt is dampening from my tears and probably my snot. I just know I need a good cry. I need to let it all out.

After twenty minutes of my hysterics, I eventually settle down, mostly from exhaustion. I glance at Chance to throw him an apologetic smile. He shakes his head, and I notice his unshed tears. Seeing the pain in his eyes makes me hold him tighter.

Taking a deep breath, I turn toward Layna's stone again.

I love you so much, Layna. You are with me always…every day and every night. You'd be proud of me because I have learned to pick up the pieces and find joy in my life again. I promise to visit you more often now. I won't wait so long. And, if you're with Duke, give him a kiss for me. Until we meet again, Layna.

I gesture to Chance that I'm ready to get back in my wheelchair. With a swift move, he lifts me up and places me back in my chair.

Once we drive away, Chance doesn't take me directly home. Instead, he brings me to the lake. "I'm not ready to go back yet, Lily. Is it okay if we go for a walk on the path here? It's so pretty, and I think we both need to just unwind a bit."

I nod, also not ready to go back home yet.

After walking a bit, he sits on a bench facing the lake. Once I park my wheelchair next to him, he says, "Tell me about her, Lily. I want to know."

I take a deep breath. With my device, I finally share my deepest thoughts about Layna. "She was my twin sister and my best friend. She was amazing and perfect—beautiful, smart. That's not all, though. She really did have a heart of gold. She helped everybody, especially me. She always took care of me. Protected me. Even at the end…she died protecting me." I stare off in the distance, remembering that dreaded night.

Chance reaches out to hold my hand. "What happened?"

"We were heading home from prom. Layna insisted that I be her date, even though she was asked by the most popular guy in high school. But, she said she had always wanted to go to our senior prom with me. It was a great night. We both dressed up in matching dresses, and she made sure I had the time of my life. It was my first dance, and Layna wanted it to perfect. And it was. Until we were driving home. I was in the back in my wheelchair, strapped securely. The roads were slippery, and the headlights came from nowhere. It all happened so fast. All I remember is Layna yelling, 'Hold on, Lily.' She spun the steering wheel and took the impact of the hit. Typical Layna thing to do. She turned the van in such a way so that the truck wouldn't hit me. The next time I opened my eyes, I was in the hospital. Layna was already gone. Apparently, she died on impact. And me? I barely had a scratch." It takes me a long time to say all this through my device, but it's important that I share the events of that night with somebody…with Chance.

"Lily, you can't hold this guilt inside you. I promise you, your sister would not want that."

"No, no she wouldn't. I didn't even go to her funeral. I was a mess. So many emotions were going through me—anger, depression, guilt, hate. And fear. Most of all fear. I was too afraid to face reality, so I avoided it. I didn't want to let her go, so I never said my goodbye. Until today. Thank you for taking me."

"I'm glad you asked me to take you. Thank you for telling me about Layna. Anytime you want to visit her, I'm here for you, mademoiselle." Chance stands up and bows while he takes my hand to kiss it.

Later that night, Mom says, "So, how did it go?"

I know she's talking about Layna. "It felt good to go there…and to let her go," I reply.

"I'm proud of you, honey." Mom smiles, but I notice her eyes sparkling with tears.

Dad says, "You've been spending a lot of time with Chance. I like him and all, but what's going on with you guys?"

Leave it to Dad to be direct.

"We're just friends." I shrug my shoulders, hoping he will drop the subject. Truth is, I have avoided thinking about my feelings toward Chance.

"Yes, we see you guys are becoming very close. We just don't want you to get hurt, honey," Mom chimes in.

"Everybody gets hurt," I reply. I can't hide forever in a sheltered life for fear of being hurt. I now realize that my parents and Layna have protected me my entire life. I have to grow up at some point and face the world—the good and the bad.

"Okay, Lily, fair enough. But, if he even thinks about hurting you, I swear he'll have to deal with me." I guess some habits die hard. Dad will always remain protective of me.

Curve Balls

Creating Memories

Chapter Eleven

During my last year in college, Chance and I spend almost every day together. If we don't see each other, we text and catch up on our day. I don't hold anything back from him anymore. Completely trusting him, I allow myself to be me without focusing on my disabilities.

One evening, Chance comes over and we watch a movie in my room. While I watch it from my wheelchair, he lounges on the recliner, drinking his Coke. As he's about to take another sip, suddenly the glass slips out of his hand.

"Shit! Damn it!" He opens and closes his hand quickly, as if testing it.

"What happened?" I ask.

Still shaken up, Chance remains silent.

"It's no big deal. It can be cleaned up," I try to assure him since he seems very distraught.

Chance shakes his head, as if trying to focus.

"What's wrong, Chance? Why are you so upset?"

He continues to ignore me but mumbles, "I'll clean it up."

Once everything is clean, he sits back down in the recliner. I can see the distressed look still in his eyes, which worries me. He has never acted like this.

"Is there something you want to talk about, Chance? Why are you upset about dropping the glass?"

"Nah, it's all good. Listen, Lily, I'm really tired tonight. I think I'm going to head out and call it a night."

Without saying another word—without even glancing my way—Chance rushes out of my room.

The incident isn't brought up again until the next time something happens. A few months later, Chance and I are walking by the lake. As I'm driving my wheelchair, Chance is being his usual self, running to the lake and throwing pebbles to make them bounce in the water. He runs back to me after the toss and says, "Did you see that? I swear I made it bounce four times. I'm becoming a professional at this!"

"Maybe you should compete professionally." I can't help but tease him.

"Yeah! Maybe I can be the champion of making my pebbles bounce the most! My name can be listed in the Guinness Book of Records!"

We both laugh, enjoying the spring weather.

"It's all about picking the right pebble and twisting that wrist just the perfect way. Here! Watch this!" Chance runs back to the lake and tosses another pebble. This one bounces three times. "See that?"

In his excitement, he turns toward me and starts sprinting back. As soon as he takes a few steps, though, his legs give out from under him. In a split second, Chance has fallen down to his knees. As if shocked himself, he lowers himself down all the way and sits on the grass. He places his head in his hands, trying to get his bearings.

"Are you okay? What happened? Did you trip?" I wouldn't normally worry about a trip, but his reaction to it has me terrified. He simply sits there and stares at the sky in distress without saying a word.

"Talk to me, Chance. Are you hurt?" Since he hasn't answered me, I contemplate calling for help. Why is he behaving this way? His knees literally just buckled. Maybe it was the way he turned quickly. Wishing that I can get off this stupid wheelchair and check on him myself, I finally say, "I'm calling for help."

As if that brings him back to the present, Chance turns his attention toward me. He then moves his legs up and down, testing them. When satisfied, he slowly tries to stand up, making sure his legs can support him. Taking one guarded step at a time, he cautiously approaches me.

"I'm okay. Let's go by that bench for a bit," Chance says, his voice thick with distress.

I follow him, knowing something is dreadfully wrong.

Once sitting, he takes some deep breaths, staring out into the distance. I don't dare say a word, knowing he needs some time to fight whatever battles he's fighting.

Without looking at me, he says, "My father died of ALS when I was 21. My mom killed herself a year later."

I shut my eyes, hoping I heard him wrong.

"He died a horrible death. My mom and I watched him helplessly as he slowly deteriorated. He used to be a powerful man. He was a Lieutenant in the U.S. Army, so it was very hard psychologically for him to accept what was happening to him. Mom and I took care of him—helped him with everything. He hated it. He would beg us to end it for him. He would even point to his gun when he was nearing the end."

I hold my breath, not wanting to interrupt him.

Chance sighs, rubbing his face. "Of course, we never did. We hated what was happening to him, but how could Mom and I just end his life? No matter how much he begged, we let him suffer. He died slowly and painfully."

He turns to me and reaches for my hand. I put my other hand on top of his, encouraging him to continue.

"We didn't have the guts to do it, Lily. After he died, Mom went into depression. She couldn't deal with the guilt and couldn't let go of what her strong, powerful husband went through at the end. She started worrying about me, confessing that ALS ran on my dad's side. Although familial ALS is not common, the risks for me were much higher suddenly. She insisted that I go through the genetic testing for it. I was young and confused. I wasn't sure whether I wanted to know or not. I finally gave in because I knew she needed to know."

Chance pulls his hand away and brushes it through his hair. I watch helplessly at his trembling hands, and he once again stares off into the distance.

"They found that gene, Lily. I have that mutated gene that runs in my family." He clears his throat. "I had to tell my mom. She was devastated...so much that she couldn't get past it. I have no idea what made her do it. I don't know if she didn't want to watch me suffer, or she didn't want to go through it all again. Either way, she did to herself what she couldn't do to her husband. I had just started medical school at that time. I came home one evening to find her body. She had shot herself with my father's gun."

No matter how hard I try to stay strong, the tears stream down my face. It's breaking my heart, shocked at what I'm hearing.

"I was lost. I had no idea what was happening around me. I

dropped out of medical school. Soon, I sold the house and just left. I literally got in my car and drove away. Away from the horrible memories, away from the pain. I just said goodbye to that life. Somehow, I ended up here in Michigan. I have no idea what brought me here. I got an apartment and enrolled in nursing school. My parents had a good amount of money that helped me through school. Once I started working, I decided I wasn't going to give up on my dreams of being a neurologist. I didn't have any ALS symptoms, so I decided to never think about my past again and look ahead toward my goals. Why not? After all, I felt healthy as a horse.

"So, I started taking classes at the college and immediately, I noticed you. Maybe I was drawn to you initially because I admired you. Maybe I wanted to get to know to you because of my past...or even my future. I noticed how beautiful you were, but your eyes were always sad. I don't know, Lily. I made up my mind that I had to know you. I wanted to know your story. I just didn't expect to get this close to you."

Finally, I ask, "Why didn't you ever tell me?"

"I have never talked about my past to anybody. I don't want to. And, I never will bring it up again. I didn't even want to bring up this whole ALS thing with you. I certainly don't think about it. I'm going to continue living my life, you know?"

I don't say anything simply because I have no idea what to say. I can't even wrap my brain around all this information.

"First time, I kind of freaked out was when I dropped that glass in your room. Then right now, when my knees just buckled from under me, I was shaken up. Both times, though, I've recovered quickly. I feel like myself again."

"Are you seeing an ALS specialist?"

"No, nor do I want to. Just not ready for that bullshit in my life right now."

Has he lost his mind? He should be getting some sort of treatment, or at the very least, he should be monitored closely.

"Listen, Lily. I know I've bombarded you with a lot of information right now, but I might as well tell you everything." Chance takes a deep breath. "I've been accepted to Johns Hopkins Medical School. They have one of the top neurology programs in the nation. I think this is my calling. No, scratch that—I *know* this is my calling. I want to be involved with research. Hey, you never know, maybe I'll even discover something amazing that can help people like you and me." Chance chuckles under his breath.

In the meantime, I try to process this new information he has just thrown at me. What exactly is he saying? Is he leaving?

"I have accepted, Lily. I'll leave at the end of the summer."

My heart already has broken today from the news of his ALS. Can it break again when there's nothing left to break? Maybe this is not real. Maybe this is just a horrible nightmare.

I look around me, trying to remember when I had fallen asleep in my room and started having this dream. Maybe if I give it some time, I'll wake up. I close my eyes, soaking in everything around me. I can hear the birds singing, the rustling of the leaves from the soft wind, and even the scurrying of a squirrel that must be nearby. Grinding my teeth, I pry my eyes open, hoping to be back in my room. I swallow the lump in my throat when I see Chance staring at me intently, waiting for me to say something.

"I'd like to go home now." I don't know what else to say. Maybe I shouldn't leave Chance alone. After all, he has just poured his heart out to me about the horrific tragedies in his life. Yet, I don't want to be near him at the moment. I can't get hold of my emotions, still in shock with all that he has shared with me.

Chance inhales a shaky breath. Without saying anything further, he walks toward the parking lot.

Chapter Twelve

A s I lie in my bed at night, I think about the last year and a half. Chance—one of the strongest people I know—has the mutated gene for ALS. Does that mean he'll get ALS? Or will he be spared? How fast will this disease progress? The thought of him bound to a wheelchair, unable to take care of himself, breaks my heart. Not him, please God, not him.

When I remember the tragic ordeal about his parents, a tremor runs up and down my spine. Visualizing Chance helping to take care of his father all those years and then finding his mom's body shatters me into pieces. I can't imagine the emotional trauma that he has held inside him all these years.

And he's leaving. He's packing his bags and riding off into the sunset. How can I possibly look out for him? How can he just leave like that? Am I being selfish? He said he needs to do this. I'm not surprised that he has been accepted into Johns Hopkins. The man is brilliant. Why shouldn't he pursue his dreams? He owes me nothing. Nothing at all.

Unable to fall asleep, I get up out of my bed and into my wheelchair to research ALS. Although I know it's a progressive disease, I don't know much more than that.

Two hours later, I'm even more depressed. There is no cure. The damn disease affects the motor function. If Chance gets diagnosed with ALS, he will become weaker and weaker until he is completely wheelchair bound and eventually confined to bed. He will be paralyzed and will require total care in everything. Even his muscles for eating will stop working, and he'll require a g-tube. Eventually, his respiratory muscles will fail, and he will have difficulty with simply breathing. I bite my lower lip hard, drawing blood, as I envision Chance in that position. God, please let there be a mistake.

Why him?

Thinking about life expectancy with people with ALS has my entire body trembling. Most people die within two to five years from the time of the diagnosis. There are very small percentages of people who do live over twenty years after diagnosis. Although there is no cure, there are some medications that can slow down the progressions of ALS. Should he be taking these?

Tomorrow, we don't see each other at the college, but he normally stops by in the evenings. Right now, I can't worry about him leaving. I have to first focus my attention on making sure he's receiving all the help he needs for ALS. I plan on confronting him tomorrow when he comes over.

The next day comes and goes. Not only does Chance not come over in the evening, but he doesn't even text. This is the first time I haven't heard from him all day in over a year. Should I be worrying about him? Is he okay?

I debate texting him myself to check on him. Convinced that I'm being paranoid, I decide to wait until the following day when I'll be seeing him at the college.

To my disappointment, Chance doesn't meet me at our usual spot the next day. Worried sick about him, I take deep breaths to try to think rationally. As my anxiety increases, I weigh out my options. Did he attend his classes today?

I decide to drive toward his next class to see if I can find out if he's even here. As soon as I turn the corner, I see him immediately. He's standing with a crowd of students, laughing and talking. Not surprised that he has captured the crowd with his charismatic personality, Chance appears to be everybody's center of attention.

Having no desire to go near that crowd, I quickly turn my wheelchair around and drive away. I guess I've been worried for no reason because Chance seems absolutely fine. Not only is he fine, he seems to be having a good old time with his friends.

Confused at why he hasn't made any effort to see me, I drive to my next class. I purposefully push any thoughts of Chance away because, at this point, nothing makes any sense.

That night, I wait anxiously for him to either stop by or text me. I stare at my device, willing it to beep as it does when I receive a text. I should text him and just find out what's going on with him. I just can't seem to do it, though. I wouldn't even know what to say.

Maybe he thinks spending time with me now is useless since he'll be leaving in a few months anyway. Summer break is almost here, after all. Maybe this is how Chance works. When he's done, he's done. After all, he did just pack up and leave his hometown.

Trying to think rationally, I convince myself that perhaps he simply needs a couple of days to himself. Maybe actually talking about everything has freaked him out. He said he had never shared any of it with anybody. Now that I know, it probably makes it all too real for him. Yes, that must be it. He just needs a few days to himself to sort it all out.

The few days become an entire week. Chance continues to avoid me. As a matter of fact, I've noticed that he purposefully takes different routes to evade me at school. Frustrated, I can't take it anymore.

On Tuesday the following week, I wait by his car in the parking lot at the time I know he leaves. Sitting in my wheelchair with my chin up and my lips set in a firm line, I'm determined to confront him.

When Chance sees me as he approaches his car, he stops in his tracks. Gathering his composure quickly, he starts walking toward me again until he stops right in front of me.

I look up directly into his eyes, trying to read him. His eyes are guarded, though, and I have no idea what he's thinking.

"Are you serious? You're going to just pretend that we haven't been friends for the last year and a half? Like we don't even know each other? Sorry, buddy, but you don't get off that easily. You owe me an explanation, and it better be a good one. I've shared some of my deepest secrets with you. You've been my best friend, and I finally permitted myself to trust you. You don't just get to walk away when you're done. That's not how life works, Chance!"

After staring at me for a few seconds, he says, "You had a lot to say there, Lily. Did you program all that in your device ahead of time?"

I can't help but smile. "Yes, last night."

Chance laughs. "Oh, how I've missed you, Lily. I purposefully stayed away because I just thought that's what you wanted. After I told you everything, you looked so upset. I wouldn't blame you one bit. I know it was a lot, and I refuse to bring my burden to you."

"Of course, it was a lot! But can I get a minute to think before you jump to conclusions?" I respond.

"You didn't even text me. You could have just contacted me. When I didn't hear from you, I knew I had to do the right thing and stay away from you." Chance kneels in front of me.

"You're a fool."

"Yes, I am." Chance leans toward me and kisses my cheek. "I've been miserable this past week without talking to you. Look at us; we're a mess."

"Speak for yourself. I'm not a mess. I know exactly who I am and what I want."

Chance smiles. "I guess I'm the messed up one. Can't argue with that. You've always been the stronger one between us."

I wouldn't have agreed to that statement a week ago. Now that I know this new information about him, though, I see that Chance needs more help than he even realizes. He's not the strong, secure guy that I had thought all this time. He's lost, confused, and hides from all his problems. The happy-go-lucky Chance that I've gotten to know has been merely a facade. Chance is not ready to deal with his past or his future.

It's like old times again for the rest of the school year. Chance and I are inseparable. I realize that when Chance can't deal with something, he likes to ignore it. I've learned through the years that this doesn't work. The best way to deal with something is to face it. It simply won't go away by avoiding it.

While Chance and I are hanging out on my back porch one day, I say, "I know what I want for a graduation present from you."

"What? I'm broke! What makes you think I was going to give you graduation gift?" Chance teases.

"Shut up. I only want one thing. Are you listening?" I ask, determined to make him focus.

"Yes, Miss Cooper. I'm all ears."

"I want you to make an appointment with an ALS specialist. I want you to be followed closely from now on. Even when you're away at medical school and I can't check on you, I want you to remember. Do it for me. That's all I want."

Chance looks away, staring at the backyard like it's the best view in the world.

"Please, Chance. It's important. Please do it for me. Promise me."

When Chance turns toward me, he sees the tears that have gathered in my eyes. Before I can stop myself, a single tear sneaks out. Chance reaches with his fingers and softly caresses it away.

"Don't, Lily. I can't bear it. And okay, I promise. I'll do it for you." Chance kisses my cheek.

"Make an appointment as soon as possible."

"Okay! Aren't you demanding! Anything else?" Chance laughs.

"That's all. Thank you." Okay, I won this battle. It's a start.

Chapter Thirteen

C hance is true to his word and starts seeing a specialist. A series of neurological tests are performed, and none of them show any indication that Chance has ALS. Although he does possess the mutated gene, he is asymptomatic. The physician does not diagnose him with the disease. He doesn't think that the episodes of dropping the glass and knees buckling are related to ALS. The physician feels that we'd see more than a couple of random episodes if he has the disease. However, he is quick to remind Chance that just because he doesn't have ALS now, it doesn't mean he won't have it in the future. The good news is that they will keep a close eye on Chance and continue to monitor him.

Of course, both Chance and I are ecstatic about the news. Chance also shares that the doctor told him if he's diagnosed with it in the future, in some rare cases, ALS can be reversible. I share his excitement and his hope. This is what I give him because this is what he needs. However, inside I remain cautiously optimistic.

When I graduate, knowing Chance is out in the crowd with my parents to support me makes it all even more worthwhile. It feels good to go across the stage to receive my diploma. I had missed my high school graduation since I had no desire to go without Layna. Today is a different day, and I'm proud of my accomplishment of graduating on time with my teaching degree.

My parents are beside themselves. Mom can't stop crying; she can barely get a word out. Even my dad is teary-eyed.

"Darling, you do realize that you've made us the proudest parents on this planet, don't you?" he asks, pulling me into his embrace.

My smile widens. Actually, I haven't stopped smiling in the last couple of hours. This is my day and damn it, I've worked my butt off for this.

Mom whispers to me, "Layna would be so proud of you, sweetie. You know that, right?"

I nod because I know Layna is right here with me. There's no way she would miss such a big event like this. Of course, she's here supporting me.

Chance comes to the house to continue the celebration with us. When we're alone in my room later, he pulls out a card and hands it to me. "Here's your graduation gift."

"You already gave me a graduation gift." I remind him of our deal.

"Here, I'll open it, smartie!" Once opened, he hands me the card, but keeps the envelope with him.

The card has a picture of a graduation cap on the front. Inside, I see Chance's writing.

Lily,

Look at you! All grown up and ready to conquer the world! There are no words to describe how I feel right now. You have been my hero from the first day I met you. Thank you for being my best friend, my family, my everything.

Now, go find a job!

Love,
Chance

I can't help but laugh at his last sentence. He can never stay serious for too long. I hold my arms open for him for a hug. Chance leans toward me, and I pull him into my arms.

"Thank you." This time I use my own words. I know they don't sound perfect, but Chance knows me well enough to understand what I'm saying to him.

"You're welcome," Chance says. "Oh, and I have one more thing." His eyes filling with excitement, Chance hands me the envelope. He pulls tickets out and places them in front of me.

Confused and curious, I squint my eyes to see what it says. They are two first class airline tickets from Michigan to Cancun.

"I'm taking you to Cancun for your gift, Lily. We're staying there for a week! I already talked it over with your parents, and I thought maybe we can take your manual, folding wheelchair so it'll be easier to get around. Your communication device can still attach to it. I've researched everything. The resort is handicapped accessible and so are the beaches! We can even use one of their wheelchairs with big wheels that can go right to the ocean! I'm so psyched about this trip!" Chance is rambling with excitement, smiling from ear to ear.

"Who's going to help me there?" Staying with him for a week is out of the question. I have to be fed, bathed, and even cleaned up after using the bathroom.

"Me! I can help you with everything! It's not a big deal."

"But, it's a big deal to me," I reply. I don't want to be upset about this because I know he means well. I can see the enthusiasm in his eyes, but it's another reminder of our circumstances.

"Lily, you know that I'm a nurse, right?" Chance teases.

"But I'm not your patient! I'm not your patient! I want you to see me as your equal, not your fragile patient who needs to be taken care of!" By now, I'm furious! How can he not know how I feel? I fight the tears from sneaking out. Quickly turning my wheelchair away from him, I try to put some distance between us.

Taking a deep breath, Chance says, "I've never thought of you as my patient, Lily. I'm sorry if I made you feel that way just now. I've always seen you as my equal, but that doesn't mean I don't like to take care of you. I like helping you. Why does that make me a bad guy? What's wrong with me wanting to help someone I care about?"

"Forget it! You won't understand!"

"Try me."

"People have to do everything for me. I hate it. It makes me feel dependent, helpless. I don't want you to see me that way."

"One thing you're not is helpless, Lily. For God's sake, you just graduated with honors from a very prestigious college!"

"I need help with basic functions. Putting on clothes, bathing, eating…it sucks, Chance! And I don't want your help."

"Fine, I don't understand it, but I'll give in. How about if we have your personal helper come with us? If she's not available, we'll find somebody else. Remember, the vacation is for you and me, though. That's my last week before I leave for medical school. I planned the dates accordingly. I want to have the time of our lives before I have to leave. So your helper is only there to assist you with your needs. That doesn't mean she goes everywhere we go. Deal?"

Chance uses his stern voice, but I catch the smirk he tries to hide.

"Deal," I say, smiling smugly.

"It's time for your stretching and exercises. Are you ready?"

"No, none of that today. I want a break. It's my graduation day, after all."

"Uh, nope! No breaks. We work out every day whether you like it or not." Chance folds his arms in front of him, ready for this next battle. "I've worked you out every single day for the last year. I'm taking a lot of pride on how relaxed your muscles are. I'd like to think I had something to do with that. We're not going to quit now. Not to mention, I gave in to you about bringing a third wheel on our vacation. So you owe me this! Besides, I know you love the massages."

"That's because you have healing hands." I do love his massages. My muscles just melt under his touch.

"Healing hands…hmm, I like that. I love our sessions. It gives me an excuse to touch you."

My mouth drops open as I stare at him. Did he just say that? Is he teasing me again? Chance simply shrugs his shoulders and winks.

"You're impossible," I reply.

"I'm impossibly stubborn, lassie. Just remember that."

Giving up, I transfer onto my bed and Chance sets to work.

The summer ends way too quickly. Chance and I spend every day together. If we're not together, we're texting about nothing and everything. Chance and I avoid talking about ALS unless something comes up. And, I purposefully avoid thinking about the fact that he'll be leaving soon.

He takes me to visit Layna regularly. I tell her all of my deepest secrets, including my fears of losing Chance.

That summer, I also land a job at Marygrove College. They hire me full-time, assisting in some classes as a teacher's assistant and also to be involved with a research project with a well-known professor. He is working on developing the most modern assistive technologies to help people with various disabilities. This job is perfect for me because nothing would be more gratifying than helping to make somebody's life a little easier. I'm also able to pursue a Master's Degree in Education Technology. This will probably help me specialize in using technology with the special needs population.

Before leaving for our Cancun trip, Chance and I plan out the details. To my relief, Lauren is able to join us. Chance has prepared well for the flight and bringing my wheelchair. This will be the first time I'll be flying since my family has never been able to afford a trip like this.

Once seated in the plane, Chance checks to ensure that my seat belt is on tight before buckling his up. Lauren has her seat a few rows behind us. I'm grateful that Chance has been able to pay for Lauren's trip as well.

As the plane takes off, my excitement, combined with nervousness, builds. I stare out of the window, smiling wide. Chance grabs my hand and squeezes it. When I turn toward him, he throws me a quick wink. Soon, we're up in the air and into the open sky, making me feel like I'm on top of the world.

Chance leans toward me and asks, "Happy?"

I smile, squeezing his hand.

"You know your dad pulled me aside to talk to me before we left?"

Surprised, I question him with my eyes since I can't access my communication device. Chance has gotten very good at reading my body language and my expressions. It's almost like he can read my mind.

"Yeah, he said, and I quote, 'That's my baby, Chance. She's never been too far away from me. You make sure you take good care of her, you hear?'"

I giggle.

Chance laughs with me. "So I said, 'Sir, I will protect her with my life.'"

I roll my eyes at his dramatic reply. I think my father will always think of me as a baby, even though I am almost twenty-three years old already.

He laughs some more and kisses my cheek. "I'm happy, too," he whispers.

When we land, the shuttle picks us up. While Chance carries me to a seat in the shuttle, Lauren folds my wheelchair and stores it in the back. It's already late evening, but my heart flutters with excitement as I smell the tropical breeze. As soon as we reach the resort, the friendly staff pampers our every need. They're already waiting for us with drinks and carry our luggage to our rooms.

Never been too far from home, let alone out of the country, I'm in awe. The architect and the ethnicity of the place make me want to go exploring, even though I'm exhausted. The Mexican music playing in the background rejuvenates me. I know it's late, though, so we head straight upstairs to our rooms.

Chance has both of us booked into a two-bedroom suite, while Lauren has her own separate room. Lauren already knows to come into my bedroom in the mornings to help with my bathing and toiletry. Because of the way my life has been through the years, my body is actually trained to use the bathroom on a specific schedule.

Most people would probably not give using the bathroom a second thought. For me, though, this process is very stressful unless I have a plan. Luckily, Lauren knows my schedule very well, so she'll make sure to be available to help me.

Chance has seen me eat plenty of times, so I'm not too worried about going out to eat with him here. Truth be told, Chance probably understands my body very well. He has attended many of my therapy sessions, not to mention, working with my body every single day during our exercise sessions. Chance knows my limitations and has accepted them. So, before coming on this trip, I promised myself not to worry about anything, but to focus on my restricted time with him. I want this week to be special for both of us. After all, neither of us knows what the future has in store for us. My entire life, I've been forced to plan everything—how to get around, who will be picking me up, when to eat. This week, I make a conscious decision to live for the moment.

Chance has purposefully picked a resort that's more secluded to avoid too much crowd. When we reach our suite, I can't help but scream in delight. It's an oceanfront room with a spectacular view of the mass body of water. The décor of the suite is also a Mexican theme with beautiful, bright colors and arched doorways. Besides the two bedrooms, the suite also has a sitting room and a small kitchen. I inhale the refreshing ocean scent and smile when I hear the waves crashing on the shore. Watching my reaction, Chance simply laughs with me.

"I love seeing you this happy, Lily."

Happy? No, I'm ecstatic!

We decide to order room service since it's already late, and we'll have a long day tomorrow. After helping me eat and use the bathroom, Lauren gets me ready for the night. I'm happy to see that the bathroom is accessible to help me with my needs.

"Do you need anything else, Lily?" Lauren asks once she changes me to my tank top and shorts and places me back in my wheelchair. When I smile and shake my head, she squeezes my hand. "Lily, Chance is really special. And, he cares about you...like a lot. Make this week count, okay?" I smile and nod. I can always count on Lauren to tell me what's on her mind.

Once Lauren goes to her own room, Chance helps me to my bed and works on my muscles. I may whine and complain to him, but I actually love the way it makes me feel when he works on me. They fatigue throughout the day, which makes me even tighter. Sometimes, my calves cramp from lack of movement. Luckily, Chance can get deep into the muscle bellies, and he magically takes all the pain away.

"You know you always complain when I make you do this, but I bet you'll miss it once I'm gone." I know Chance is trying to tease me, but suddenly the reality of him leaving next week hits home. I quickly turn my head to the side, not wanting him to see my pain.

Chance lies down next to me. "I shouldn't have said that. I promised myself that I wouldn't think about me leaving...at least not when I'm here with you. I just want us to enjoy each other without worrying about anything else. I'm sorry, Lily. I didn't think."

I roll toward him and reach my hand to touch his face. Of course, it was an innocent statement, but I've purposefully avoided thinking about it.

Chance plays with my hair. "I love your hair, Lily. And even more, I love your eyes. They're the most unusual shade of green. Do you know that only 2% of the population worldwide has green eyes? You know what that means? You're even more unique than you realized."

I can't help but laugh.

"I'm too tired to walk to my bedroom, Lily. I'm sleeping right here. You okay with that?"

I've never had anybody sleep in the same bed as me besides Layna. I definitely never had a guy share my bed. If I'm honest with myself, though, I don't want him to leave. Without analyzing it further, I scoot closer to him.

Chance pulls me into his arms and holds me in his embrace the entire night.

It doesn't feel strange. There's no tension.

Instead, it feels like home.

The week with Chance flies by with a blink of an eye. We spend the majority of our time at the beach. The wheelchairs provided there have very large wheels and can easily be pushed on the sand. Even so, there's a ramp that goes all the way into the ocean.

I have never seen an ocean before—at least not in person. I lose myself in its mystic. There is no end to it. It just simply disappears into the horizon. I can almost taste the salt in the air as the ocean breeze fans my hair. The rippling of the waves creeping up on my feet just adds to the feeling of pure bliss.

Chance picks me up and carries me into the infinite body of water. "You need to swim in the ocean, my dear Lily, not just those controlled therapy pools." Although fear of the unknown encloses me, I've never felt freer. We both laugh as the waves crash into us. I hang onto him with all my might, and we both lose ourselves in the ecstasy the mysterious ocean brings us.

If we're not in the ocean, we're in the pool or in our lounging chairs, drinking mai tais or Piña coladas. Since I rarely drink, a couple of drinks during the day is more than enough for me. I even permit him to feed me and help me with the drinks. I figure life is too short to worry about little things like that. If he's comfortable with it, why am I making such a big deal about it? It's my own issue, and I make a conscious decision to put it away for now.

When we decide to share a drink, Chance says, "Wow, that's almost like kissing."

Completely taken aback, I almost choke.

"You know, that's the closest we've come to kissing," Chance continues as if it's the most natural thing to say.

"What?" I finally respond, shocked at the direction of this conversation.

"Okay, I take it back. Kissing would be a lot more fun."

Chance winks and takes another sip.

I can feel the heat rising in my cheeks. Why does he insist on putting me in these awkward situations? I know he's getting a kick out of it.

"I love watching your face turn red while you try to hide your eyes from me. I just can't help but tease you, if for nothing else than to watch your reaction."

I have no response for him but to stick my tongue out at him like a child, which causes him to burst out laughing.

"I'm glad I'm entertaining you," I respond with my device, rolling my eyes.

"Oh, you are definitely entertaining, sweet Lily."

I smile, as pure happiness fills me, dreading when the week will be over.

I have never felt freer than I do this week. This week with him makes me believe that anything is possible, even if the feeling is short lived since neither of us is ready to face reality.

So, all week long, we laugh. And, we laugh some more.

The nights are filled with strong arms holding me, making me feel safe and secure. Every night after doing my stretches, Chance sleeps in my bed with me. There's no explanation, no awkwardness. It feels so right that he is there, right next to me.

On our last night, after Lauren showers me and helps me get ready for bed, I stay up longer with Chance, not wanting our vacation to end just yet. Before he puts me in bed, I know I have to get some things off of my chest.

"I want to talk for a bit first," I tell him with my device.

"Okay, what's up?"

"I know we promised not to ruin our vacation by talking about unpleasant things, but I have to talk to you. I'm scared, Chance."

Chance takes a deep breath and sits down on the bed.

"I'm scared about that mutated gene for ALS. I'm scared that you won't ask for help if you need it after you leave. And, I'm scared of what's going to happen after you leave. You know, with our friendship."

Chance waits a second before answering. "I'm scared too, Lily," he finally whispers.

"Thank you for bringing me here. I'll forever cherish our time here."

Chance stands up and leans down in front of my wheelchair.

"Me, too. You have no idea how much this week has meant to me." He pauses and then stands back up. "Okay, enough of this serious stuff. Time for your exercises."

I'm not surprised at all that he's ready to move to a different topic. That's what Chance does. He can't face anything head on. He'd rather pretend everything is great, and if he avoids things hard enough, somehow these things will just disappear.

I sigh, knowing the conversation is done.

After the workout, both Chance and I lie on the bed, neither of us saying a word. Finally, Chance turns to me and pulls me into his arms. Not wanting to ruin this moment, I sink into his embrace, knowing that his scent, his strong arms, the feel of his hard body against mine, and the beating of his heart will forever be etched in my memory.

For the next hour, I force myself to relax my body, hoping to fall asleep. When I finally settle myself down, I hear Chance say, "You still awake?"

I decide not to answer immediately, curious about why he asked me.

"Guess you fell asleep. I can't sleep, Lily. There's so much I want to say to you. Maybe it'll be easier to say it since you can't hear me." Chance takes a deep breath. Just as I'm about to let him know that I'm awake, he continues. "Lily, I wish our circumstances were different. I wish I wasn't leaving or you could come with me or something. You have no idea how much I care about you. A part of me wishes I would just stay. But, I can't do that, Lily. I just can't. I have to do this. I have to follow what I had set myself to do from the beginning. Am I scared? Hell, yeah, I'm scared. I wonder if this stupid ALS will just sneak up on me and who knows? I could die before medical school is even over. So my choice of going through with it really makes no sense. I just know that I can't allow ALS to control me. I refuse to live life by waiting around to see if I'll get it or not. I have to pursue my dreams. I really hope you understand that, Lily. I hope you don't resent me for leaving. It's probably one of the hardest choices I've ever had to make. You see, every day counts. We must live every day to the fullest."

Chance sighs deeply and holds me tighter. I continue to pretend I'm sleeping because I know Chance is not good with talking about his feelings.

"I don't know why I have such strong feelings for you, Lily.

I've never allowed myself to get this close to anybody. I'll miss you every minute that I'm away from you. Every second." Chance slowly caresses my lower lip with his thumb. Ever so tenderly, I feel his soft lips touch mine. It's a brief kiss, but I feel his every emotion flowing through it. And, with this powerful kiss, I'm helpless, as he steals my heart.

Finding Me

Courage

Chapter Fourteen

Once Chance drops me back home from our trip, he doesn't stay long. He brings my belongings into the house and gives me a quick kiss on my cheek.

"See you soon, Lily," he whispers.

I try to make eye contact, but he avoids it. He quickly shakes my dad's hand, hugs my mom, and darts out the front door without a backward glance, taking a piece of me with him.

His flight is for the next day, but Chance doesn't stop by to say goodbye. I'm not surprised at all because I know him now like the back of my hand.

I receive a text from him that says, "On the plane" and another that says, "Landed and now at the apartment. Unpacking and preparing for my classes."

I text back, "Okay, be safe."

That night, as I lie in my bed, I finally allow myself to cry for the first time. I cry for Chance and his tortured past. I cry for his unknown future. I cry that I won't be seeing him every day. I cry for the inevitable change that will occur in our relationship with time. And. most of all, I cry from feeling powerless that none of this is in my control. I'll have to watch helplessly as the future unfolds, no matter how much it kills me inside.

Of course, I don't share my feelings with anybody, especially Chance. He has made his decision and even if it hurts that he's gone, I'm proud of him. His courage of pursuing his dreams instead of feeling sorry for himself is truly inspiring. Besides, he's a brilliant man, and if given the right opportunities, I know he can be a huge asset to the medical community.

True to his word, Chance texts me every day. He fills me in on how the classes are going and that he's now seeing a physician there who was referred to him. He assures me that he has not been diagnosed with ALS still and that he's had no strange symptoms.

Lucky for me, my job starts as soon as he leaves. I bury myself in my work, needing to stay busy. The fact that I'm used to the college definitely helps make things a bit easier. I also know a lot of the faculty, so they already recognize what I'm capable of doing and show me mutual respect.

On weekends, I continue to attend my therapy sessions. It's difficult to get used to not having Chance with me, but I purposefully avoid thinking about it. My body definitely misses his daily massages and stretches. I can already tell that my muscles are becoming tighter. Sometimes, even if I'm doing nothing but lying on my bed, terrible pains radiate up and down my legs. These are the times when I crave somebody to move my legs or to massage the charley horses out of my muscles. I refuse to bother my parents with such things since they both still work hard every day. Ignoring the muscle spasms, I soon get used to the pain.

Although Chance continues to text me every day, I can tell that our conversations are changing. They're not as comfortable as they once were. It may be because we're both busy. Or it may be for the simple fact that an invisible wall has begun forming between us.

We follow each other on social media, so occasionally I notice pictures of him going out with his new friends on Facebook. He looks happy and strong. Although a big part of me is dying slowly without him, another part of me is glad he seems happy.

I, too, begin making friends soon. If my colleagues from work have a get-together or an outing, I force myself to join them. Like Chance has always said, "Live every day to the fullest."

Holidays are soon upon us. As I'm driving my wheelchair to our minivan after work one evening, I notice my dad's not in the van. That's unusual for him because he doesn't like me waiting in the cold. Just when I start sending a text to him, I hear, "Hello, Lily."

Gasping, I whirl my wheelchair around to the familiar voice. Unable to help myself, I let out a scream. Before I know it, Chance already has his arms wrapped around me.

"Damn, Lily! I've missed you! You look great!"

I can't even speak, so caught up in emotions. The tears flow freely down my cheek, and Chance tenderly wipes them away.

"I'm here for the week during the holidays. I went straight to your parents' house and took the minivan. I wanted to surprise you."

All I can do is smile in awe, praying it's not just a dream.

During the week, we catch up on everything. I tell him about my job and my new friends. He shares how he's met some phenomenal professors, and he swears that all of the students are geniuses. He says he's learning a lot and although it was tough at first, he's meeting some great people.

Although both of our lives are heading in different directions, we put that aside for the week. Once again, we are best friends as if nothing has changed. I'm happy to see that he looks so healthy and full of energy. He, in turn, is happy about my work and my new friends.

Chance stays at my parents' house during his visit, but they have him stay in the spare bedroom. Every evening, we watch our favorite movies together in my room until late night while lying in bed. Before we fall asleep, though, he goes to the spare room. He says it doesn't feel right to break my dad's rules in his house.

For Christmas, I don't have a gift for Chance since I wasn't expecting him, but when we're alone, he pulls out a small box, wrapped in gold wrapping paper.

"I wanted to get you something. Merry Christmas, Lily."

"But I have nothing for you," I say.

"I don't need anything. I've got everything I need right here in front of me," Chance replies as he winks.

"Always teasing me." I shake my head while taking the gift.

"I love teasing you. Now let's see what's in that box." Chance assists me with ripping the wrapper and opening the box.

I gasp when I see the gold heart locket in the box. The necklace sparkles in the light as he pulls it out. When he opens the locket, I see pictures of us at Cancun. One picture is when he's kissing my cheek in the pool, and the other picture is when he is carrying me in his arms in the ocean. Both are tender, happy moments we shared. I turn the locket over and see "Always" engraved on the back. Chance doesn't say anything, but takes the necklace back in his hands and puts it on me.

"Thank you," I say with my words this time. Although the

words are not said properly, I want him to hear the emotion in my voice.

"You're welcome. I'm glad you like it. Now, what movie do you want to see tonight? *Harry Potter* or *The Hunger Games?*"

Okay, that's my cue that he's ready to change the subject. Before long, I'm snuggled in his arms as we lie on the bed watching Harry Potter.

The next day, Chance leaves, whispering, "See you soon."

Unfortunately, his idea of soon is very different from my idea of soon.

Chance continues to text me, but he doesn't visit during the summer break. He has committed himself to working on a research project with one of the professors. Our texts are brief and detached. Sometimes, it almost feels like he's texting out of obligation.

I bury myself in my work and my studies. It feels good to actually receive a real paycheck. I refuse to think about Chance, although once in a while, I find myself checking his Facebook wall to see what he's been doing. Many times, I see the pictures he's been tagged in by his friends. To my relief, he looks healthy. The pictures that hurt the most are the ones of him partying with girls. Often, these girls are hanging all over him, and Chance has no problems holding them in his arms. Once there's even a picture of a beautiful girl sitting on his lap while he's laughing.

For the life of me, I have no idea why I'm slowly torturing myself. I know if I click on his page, I'll see things I don't want to see. Powerless, I purposefully continue to cause myself the pain. I can't help but be jealous. I don't know if it's because I wish I were one of the girls or because I wish I weren't a prisoner in my own wheelchair.

I know Chance and I have been best friends for a long time, but a part of me has to accept that he never really saw me as he sees these other girls. Sure, he cares about me, but he's never been attracted to me. Can I blame him? After all, he's a gorgeous man who can basically get any of those beautiful, able-bodied girls who are all over him.

Knowing I need to let him go—not only for him but also for me—I eventually stop texting him back. At first, Chance continues to try to reach me, but I don't respond. He even calls my parents to make sure I'm okay. When they assure him I'm doing fine, I receive one final email from him.

Hey, Lily,

I've been texting you quite a bit lately, but you haven't replied back. I got worried so I called your parents. They assured me that you're doing great and everything is working out well with your job and school. I wish I could be there in person so we can talk face to face about this. I just can't get out of the commitments here, though. Since you're not replying back to me, I can only assume that you don't want to put in the effort any longer to keep in touch. If I'm wrong about this, please let me know. If I don't hear back from you, I guess my assumption is correct. I'm not quite sure what to say, but if that is your desire, I respect it. Just know that whatever you may need in the future, I'll be here for you.

Always,
Chance

A single tear slowly rolls down my cheek and disappears behind my shirt.

I live my life without worrying about my past or the future. I no longer allow my disability to slow me down. After all, this is the only life I've been given. There are no second chances, so I might as well learn to work with what I have.

I become very close to Kathy Johnson, one of the faculty members. As time passes, we hang out more frequently. We eventually become close enough that I even allow her to help me with my needs. If we go out to eat together, Kathy feeds me. She learns about my wheelchair and my communication device. A few times, she even helps me to the bathroom. It doesn't seem to bother her. She simply says, "Girlfriends pee in front of each other all the time."

As I become more independent, I think about moving out and living on my own. I find a facility that is set up as an apartment complex, but it's also more like an assistive living place. Most people there need some help, whether it's total care or people like me who just need help with basic care due to physical limitations. There are twenty-four-hour nurses there in case anybody needs them. They provide their own aides to help the residents. Also, they have vans that would provide me with transportation. From my calculations, I know I can afford the rent there. The more I research it, the more I like it. I'm twenty-four years old already; it's about time I move out of my parents' home.

All hell breaks loose when I discuss my plans with my parents.

"Have you lost your mind, Lily? No way! I forbid it!" Dad yells as soon as his mind processes what I'm saying to them.

"Lily, aren't you happy with us? Why would you want to leave your home?" Mom asks, confused by my request.

"I need my own life," I say with my device. I've been expecting the resistance from my parents, so I'm prepared for this fight.

"We give you all of the freedom you want, Lily," Dad insists, pacing the floor.

"It's not far from here. You can come see me every night if you want. I need to meet new people and be on my own. Please, I'm an adult now."

"Lily, what is this about? Where is this even coming from?" Mom sits down in the chair next to me.

"I need my own life. Please, let me live it. I don't want to be a twenty-four-year-old adult still living with my parents. You have to understand that just because I'm in a wheelchair doesn't mean I'm a child. I know you are scared because you love me, but please, let me at least try this. If it doesn't work, I'll move back home. I promise to come home every weekend. I don't want my disabilities to stop me from living my life. I need your support on this." I had programmed this into my device the night before to make sure I didn't miss saying anything.

Mom and Dad look at each other. Finally, taking a deep breath, Dad says, "Let us go see the place first, Lily. Please give me time to think about it. This is very hard."

It doesn't matter how much he thinks about it. I've already made up my mind, so whether he likes it or not, I will be moving out. I don't say that to him, though, because I know it's not the right timing. Instead, I nod my head.

Chapter Fifteen

Although living on my own is scary at first, I'm proud of myself for facing my fears. Soon, I become accustomed to my life on my own. The staff is great, and they soon realize that I'm probably the smartest resident there. The other residents also get to know me pretty quickly and respect me for working full time and attending school at the same time.

Kathy comes to visit me a few times a week and so do my parents. Life is suddenly even busier for me. I travel to and from work with the transportation provided by the facility. The staff there also makes sure to bathe, toilet, and feed me. I train them well on my routine and exactly how I like things done. I'm glad that it's usually the regular caretakers who come to help me.

Every weekend, as promised, I visit my parents. Every Friday evening, Dad is right in the front, waiting to pick me up. I don't mind, though. I enjoy going home and sleeping in my bedroom. They also take me to my therapy sessions on the weekends. Keeping up with my therapy is imperative so the right muscles stay strong and the tight muscles stay loose.

Although the staff is nice at my new place, some things still bother me. There are other residents who also drive their power wheelchairs, but require supervision when they're driving. Many times, I see their wheelchairs turned off, parked in front of the television in the common room for hours. I can't even imagine sitting in front of the TV that long, without having the freedom to move about or a choice to not watch it any longer. They can't communicate, so this is how their day passes most of the time.

Jen is the one resident who is parked in front of the television almost all day. She can't talk or move her wheelchair, so she just sits there, staring at the screen. I find out that she used to be married, but her husband was abusive. One day, he beat her to a point of leaving her with a severe head injury. Since then, she's basically been unresponsive and immobile.

Curious about her, I drive my wheelchair next to her and sit with her one evening after work.

"Big Bang Theory is on, huh? I like that show a lot. Do you?" I start a conversation to get a reaction out of her.

Jen ignores me.

I continue to talk with her with my device as if I'm talking to any other person. I make an effort to spend some time with her every evening, watching whatever she's watching. She never really acknowledges me, except for one fateful day.

As I'm talking about nothing important, just to give her companionship, she suddenly reaches with her hand and touches my cheek. Shocked—because I've never seen her move any part of her body—I simply stare at her in awe. She flashes me a quick smile, takes her hand back, and resumes staring at the television once again.

Overcome with emotion, I remain frozen for a few moments. Realizing that it was her way of being grateful for being there for her, I turn my attention back to watching TV again, smiling silently. I take joy in knowing that I've made some sort of difference in Jen's life.

Staying with others with disabilities also gives me another advantage. Everything I observe, I bring back to Professor Bailey. He's basically my boss regarding the research on adapted technology. From any information I share, we try to invent a technology that would help not only the individual but also the caretakers.

I've been lucky. My assistive device that I use to communicate also controls the television in my room, accesses the internet, and can receive and send texts. Both, my power wheelchair and my communication device, have not only provided me with independence but have improved my quality of life significantly. I can't even imagine my life without technology to help me.

Unfortunately, technology can sometimes fail. I find myself in a jam when one stormy day, I'm driving my wheelchair from one building to another at the college. The blizzard has me speeding up my wheelchair so I can reach my next destination quickly.

With no warning at all, the wheelchair stops. It completely shuts down on the sidewalk in this bitter, cold temperature.

Confused, I turn my wheelchair on and off. I know the battery has been charged all night, so I'm not sure why it's not turning back on. I purposefully have my communication device covered in its case because I didn't want it to get wet outside. Now, I regret that decision because I have no access to it and can't even ask for help.

While I continue to play around with the wheelchair, I watch helplessly as the students fly by me. Don't they wonder why I'm just sitting out here in the middle of a blizzard? Not one turns to me to see if I need help. After five minutes of turning the wheelchair on and off with no success, I contemplate whether I should start yelling to get people's attention. My toes and fingers are freezing by now and the wind is really picking up. Everybody is scurrying about me, not even giving me a second glance. It feels like I'm going back to my childhood when nobody would stop by to talk to me in school. At first, I resist the urge to scream because I don't want to cause a scene. As desperation sets in, though, I know I have no choice. Pretty soon, the passing period will be over, and nobody will be out here.

Just as I'm about to start yelling for attention, I suddenly hear, "Lily? Lily, what are you doing out here?"

I turn around to see my savior, Mark Stockton. A smile of relief spreads over me when I recognize my fellow colleague and friend.

I look down at the wheels to show him to change the wheelchair into the manual mode so he can push me. Knowing immediately that something is wrong with the wheelchair, Mark quickly starts playing with it. Unfortunately, he has no idea what to do, and when he attempts to push the wheelchair, it doesn't budge. By now, I can't even feel my fingers and toes, and I'm completely covered with snow.

"I have no idea how to work this thing. Lily, but you have to get inside. I'm going to carry you in, okay? I'll send somebody for your wheelchair later."

At this point, I'm desperate to be inside somewhere warm, so I don't even resist. Mark quickly unstraps me and picks me up. Cradling me in his arms, he runs toward the building. I bury my face into his chest, hoping that I'll eventually be able to feel my hands and feet.

Once inside, he takes me to the teacher's lounge to avoid unnecessary attention. Placing me on the sofa, he swiftly pulls my gloves and shoes off. While rubbing my hands and feet, he calls Kathy to come immediately. He knows we're good friends, and she would know what to do.

Kathy comes running and immediately falls next to me. "Oh my god, Lily! What the hell happened?"

"I saw her stuck outside. Her wheelchair wasn't working. I left it outside and carried her in. I knew she needed to get somewhere warm," Mark explains.

I can't talk since I don't have my communication device. At this point though, I'm so cold and shaking like crazy that I would fail miserably if I try to use my device.

"I'm calling 911. She may have frostbite or hypothermia. Do we even know how long she was out there?" Kathy asks.

Mark shakes his head, pulling me into his arms to stop my tremors.

Through the emotional ordeal, somehow, I make a mental note to tell Professor Bailey that there needs to be a backup battery for power wheelchairs.

By the time the paramedics arrive, I'm already back to myself, and Kathy has brought my wheelchair back inside. Luckily, my vitals are normal and my toes and fingers look good, so they don't force me to go to the hospital.

Although the entire scene is quite embarrassing, I'm grateful to Mark for finding me. Once I'm in my wheelchair with my device on, I thank him properly.

"Wow, that was close. Thank you, Mark!"

"I'm just glad I happened to be there at that time. Hey, since I rescued you, does that make me a hero now?" Mark teases.

I look up to see his blue eyes twinkling and his dimples on both cheeks as he smiles. I've known Mark for the last couple of years, and we've always gotten along well. Mark appears to be in his early thirties, and I now notice how handsome he is with his blond hair, blue eyes, and those killer dimples.

"Well, you're at least my hero," I reply.

"I'll take it!" We both laugh, partly because the scary ordeal is over and partly because we know that this is a start of a good friendship.

Once in a while, I still find myself checking on Chance's Facebook page, just to make sure that he's doing well. When I'm satisfied that he still looks healthy, I purposefully avoid looking him up again for a while.

In the meantime, my social life becomes busier. Besides spending time with Kathy, Mark and I also hang out together frequently. He takes me to the movies, and he even attends my therapy sessions occasionally. He says my life is very interesting to him. I love that Mark treats me like his equal. It may be because I'm his colleague at work, and we have mutual respect for one another.

Just when I feel that I have my life on a smooth road, suddenly, the road becomes bumpy with potholes. One evening, as I'm sitting with Jen watching one of her favorite shows, I notice her turning to look at me. At first, she simply stares and blinks several times. Then, she flashes me the tiniest smile and turns back toward the television.

I continue to stare at her, wondering what she was trying to communicate with me. Just then, her head falls to the side as if she has fainted. I try to shake her but when she doesn't respond, I scream for help at the top of my lungs.

The staff comes running and immediately notices my distressed face staring at Jen. As soon as they see her not responding, they pull her out of her wheelchair. In horror, I watch helplessly as they start CPR on her.

"I can't find a pulse," somebody yells.

"Call 9-1-1!"

"She's not breathing. Get the crash cart!"

What's happening? God no, no! Please, Jen, fight!

"One, two, three, four…" Somebody has started the chest compressions.

"Get all of the residents out of here!"

I snap out of my trance and drive away from the nightmare unfolding before my eyes. I have to get out of here, desperately needing some space.

Driving my wheelchair outside, I text Mark. I have no idea what makes me contact him and not Kathy or my parents.

"Hey, can you come over? Something bad has happened here."

Mark texts back immediately. "Are you okay? I'm on my way."

Within fifteen minutes, he's there and notices immediately that I've been crying. By now, the ambulance has already taken Jen away.

"What the hell! What's wrong?" I know he's shocked because he's never seen me cry.

"Can we go up to my room?"

"Okay, let's go." Mark follows me behind my wheelchair.

Once in my room, he sees me visibly shaking. "You need to tell me what's going on. What happened to you?"

"Jen, my friend from here. She stopped breathing. I think she's dead. It happened right in front of me."

"Oh, Lily. I'm so sorry. Shit! What can I do?"

I start to cry, unable to stop myself. I'm too upset to even use my device to talk to him more. Mark simply takes me out of my wheelchair and sits me on the sofa. He positions himself next to me and pulls me into his arms. Without saying a word, he allows me to sob into his shirt. Why is life so unfair? Jen's life has been tragic and thinking about the possibility of her taking her last breath in front of me, hurts me to the core. Slowly, I drown in Mark's arms.

But, he doesn't allow it. With his soft whispers and tender caresses down my back, he gives me strength.

Eventually, I find my bearings and glance up at him apologetically. With his feather-soft hands, he wipes my tear-soaked face.

"I'm sorry you went through that, Lily. And, I'm glad I could be here to help you."

I give him a sad smile and close my eyes. I'm exhausted, and all I want to do is sleep. Before long, I fall asleep in his arms, right there on the sofa.

When I open my eyes, the sun is already shining through the window. My first thought goes to Jen. I want to find out what happened. When Mark feels me stirring, he, too, opens his eyes. I point to my wheelchair, and he picks me back up and puts me on there.

Once I have my communication device, I say, "Sorry about my behavior last night. I'm embarrassed, but thanks for being there. Couldn't have made it through the night without you."

"It's my pleasure. How are you doing?" Mark stretches his arms above his head as he yawns.

"I need to check about Jen. I'll see you at work later."

"Oh, you're kicking me out? Guess I can take the hint," Mark teases, laughing.

Smiling, I see him to the front door.

"You sure you'll be okay, Lily?" he asks, turning back toward me.

Once I nod yes, Mark leaves, closing the door behind him.

Immediately, I call for help from the front desk. When Kendra comes to my room, I'm relieved. She's one of my regular helpers, and she always shares with me the latest gossip from this place.

"How is she?" I ask.

"I'm sorry, Lily. Jen is no longer with us. God has her now."

I turn my wheelchair away furiously. Although a part of me has known that she's gone, I'm not prepared to hear it out loud. It's not fair! She didn't do anything wrong.

"They think maybe her heart just gave out on her. They don't know for sure, of course, but that's what they think," Kendra continues to explain.

I fight the tears, angry that God has once again taken an innocent life. Jen couldn't have been older than forty. She was too damn young!

"I guess it's good, Lily. She was practically comatose. I mean, what kind of life did she have? She never responded to anything. She didn't even know what was happening around her."

That's not true! She knew! She knew everything! Jen chose to not respond. That was her choice. But, I knew better because she showed me. Even before she died, she said her goodbye to me. She knew, damn it!

I want to yell and scream at Kendra. I want to tell her don't ever say that she didn't know. Instead, I go to my bedroom and wait for Kendra to get me ready for work.

That evening, the facility holds a memorial service for Jennifer Kathleen Watson. No family members attend. Jen truly was alone in this world.

The pastor is there, and people share their favorite memories of Jen. All of the memories are about her sitting in front of the TV and watching The Big Bang Theory.

I don't have the courage to say anything. A part of me doesn't want to share Jen's secret. After all, she only allowed me to see that side of her. She didn't want anybody else to know that she was aware of everything. I decide to respect her wishes.

After the service, the residents and the staff go outside. Each of us is given a helium balloon to release at the same time, in memory of Jen. At the count of three, we all release our balloons and they soar high in the sky. There are about fifty balloons—yellow, purple, green, pink, blue, orange, red—which come together in one bunch as they fly into the abyss. As they become smaller and smaller, and eventually disappear, I say my final goodbye to Jen.

Thank you for trusting me to be your friend, Jen. I will miss spending time with you. I hope you find your peace. Be happy and fly free, my friend.

Chapter Sixteen

They say, "What doesn't kill you will only make you stronger." Life can really test one's sanity and will to survive through the most difficult times.

When none of my usual helpers come to assist me with bathing and getting ready for bed one evening, I can't help but be apprehensive. Instead, an unfamiliar aide, named Kenny, enters.

"Hi! You must be Lily. I'll be helping you out today because I guess they're short staffed. They called my agency for extra help."

Kenny appears to be in his forties with long dark hair and dark eyes. In the past, I have had male assistants, and although at first I've felt uneasy, they've always been very professional. Kenny seems polite enough, so I make a conscious effort to put aside my irrational feelings of apprehension.

"Okay, from the notes I received about you, it said that you can just tell me what you need to be done, right?"

"Yeah, I need to eat and then use the bathroom. After the shower, I'll need your help to change into my pajamas and to get ready for bed," I reply with my device.

"Perfect! No problem," Kenny says, smiling. We head to the kitchen and Kenny warms up the food. After helping me eat, Kenny follows me into the bathroom and transfers me to the adapted toilet seat. Giving me privacy, he leaves the bathroom. A short time later, he places me in the shower chair to give me a shower.

"I hear you're in school and have a full-time job. That's awesome!" Kenny continues to talk about indifferent topics while he cleans me up.

I appreciate that he's being quick about showering me and making it comfortable for me by talking about neutral subjects.

Once he's finished cleaning me, he wraps me up in the bath towel and brings me to my bedroom. "Okay, almost done. Do you need anything else before I put you in bed?"

I point toward my pajamas.

"Oh, yes, of course! We should put your nightie on, huh?" Kenny grabs the pajamas and swiftly helps put them on me. Once I'm dressed, he says, "There you go. Are you ready to go to your bed now? Do you want to drink water or anything first?"

I shake my head no. It's only nine o'clock, so it's a bit early for me to go to bed. Lately, though, I've been going to sleep at this time, having no desire to stay up. I still haven't been able to accept Jen's death, and sleeping helps control the thoughts that haunt me in my waking hours.

"Okay." Kenny helps me get to my bed. "So I guess you can't talk without your device, huh? It's cool they make things like that."

I smile. Normally, before leaving, I'm handed the switch that's attached to the wall. That way, if I need help in the middle of the night, all I have to do is push it, and somebody comes in my room to check on me. I point to the switch to remind him.

"Oh, okay, I won't forget," he says. "You know, you are a beautiful girl. Has anybody ever told you that?"

I frown because suddenly he's making me feel uncomfortable.

"Your beautiful dark hair against that flawless skin...and those eyes of yours are mesmerizing."

I try to smile politely but by this time, I just want him to leave. It's completely inappropriate for him to talk to me like this, and I plan on reporting him at the first opportunity.

"I take care of a lot of people. I've been a certified nursing assistant for over fifteen years now. I've met some great people...and beautiful ladies like you."

To my horror, his hand touches my cheek. I turn my face away and yell at him. I want him to know that he's out of line.

Kenny laughs. "It's just that you're so damn tempting. I try to fight the urges, Lily. I swear I do. But, when I take care of somebody who's as pretty as you, well, it's kind of hard to resist. Have you ever been with a man, Lily? I can make you feel good—real good."

I attempt to roll away from him and try to shout as loud as I possibly can. Before I succeed, he puts his hand over my mouth to stifle my scream. Horrified, I swing my arms wildly, hoping I can aim them accurately to hurt him.

"Man, you're feisty, aren't you? I love your spirit, Lily." Kenny laughs even louder and easily holds my arms down. Before I can react, he's suddenly on top of me. His hand remains over my mouth, and now it's impossible for me to make any noise. Scared out of my mind, I thrash my body around. To my horror, he holds me even tighter.

Before I can process anything further, his hand is under my shirt and suddenly on my breast. "Relax, Lily. Doesn't that feel good?" He plays with my nipples, going from one breast to another.

Why is this happening? As the room spins, suddenly nausea creeps up on me. I swing my arms, and a couple of times, my strikes land hard.

But, it just makes him even more aggressive. "You bitch. Keep at it, and I'll make it really hurt."

If only I can control my body more, maybe I may be able to fight him better. Feeling completely helpless, the tears roll down my face.

Kenny ignores the tears. "Don't even think about telling anybody. Nobody would believe you anyway. They would all just think you're retarded. Besides, I'm not going to penetrate you so there will be no evidence. I'm not that stupid. We're just going to enjoy each other's body. Now, stop your damn crying and be thankful that I'm willing to give you this pleasure."

God, please show me some mercy. If I can't fight this guy, please just let me pass out until this horrible nightmare is over.

Even though I continue to struggle, Kenny is already unzipping his pants. I close my eyes, wondering what sins I have committed to land me in this position.

Somewhere far off in the distance, I hear a familiar sound that my brain can't quite register. I focus hard on the sound and realize that somebody is knocking on my door. Kenny must have heard it too because he lies very still.

"Hello?" Kathy's voice echoes around us as she continues to knock on the door. "Lily? Can you tell your helper to come open the door? They just told me downstairs that he's still helping you."

Kenny doesn't make a sound, but I struggle to get free even harder, desperate to save myself.

"Lily? Are you still getting bathed? I can just go downstairs and tell them to let me in, then." There are some guests who can come to my room whenever they please. Both of my parents' and

Kathy's names are on that list.

"Hold on, please," Kenny yells. He jumps off of me and whispers, "I'm going to let her in. You better not say anything to her or I swear I will kill you both. Don't you underestimate me!"

Scared out of my wits, I nod my head.

He fixes my shirt and my hair so it doesn't look disheveled and zips his pants back up. Quickly scanning the room, he heads toward the front door to open it.

I hear Kathy say, "Oh, hi. You must be Kenny. They told me downstairs that you were in here helping Lily. You're not one of the regulars."

"No, I just come in as needed. They must have been short-staffed today, so they called my agency for extra reinforcement," Kenny explains, sounding very professional.

"Where's Lily? I wanted to visit with her."

"She's already in bed. She said she was pretty tired, so I doubt that she's in the mood for company," Kenny answers.

Oh no! Is he trying to get rid of her? Should I scream? But I don't want him to hurt Kathy. No, I have to scream. I can't have him near me again.

"Oh, I don't care. I'll wake her up if she's asleep. You know what? You can leave now, Kenny. I can finish up here."

"Uh, well, that's okay but this is my job," Kenny says, sounding frazzled.

"I won't tell anybody. No worries. Thanks again!" Kathy must have shoved him out because I hear the door close. "Lily, I can't wait to tell you this great news! I had to come here personally to share it!"

Kathy strolls into my room, and as soon as she sees the fear in my face, she runs to me. "What's wrong? What happened?" Immediately, she knows that something terrible has taken place.

I shake my head, not wanting to discuss it right now. I'm terrified of Kenny, and I don't want him to come back and hurt us. For all I know, he may be right outside. With my eyes wide, I stare at the door.

Kathy must have figured something out because she runs back to the door and puts the bolt on. The staff has the key only for the bottom lock but not the top bolt. She quickly transfers me into my wheelchair and gives me my communication device. "Talk to me, Lily. What happened?"

I shake my head, too scared to respond.

"What can I do? Should I call Mark? Your parents?"

Dad, yes! I need my daddy! Tears gather in my eyes when I think about my parents. I've never needed them more than I do at this moment.

"Parents," I manage to say with my device.

"Do you want me to call them?"

I nod. I take deep breaths to steady myself so I can use my device accurately. "Don't say anything. Just tell them I want to come home tonight and if they could pick me up."

"Okay, okay. I'm really worried about you. I know something is terribly wrong, Lily." Kathy dials my parents' phone with her cell phone. She's known my parents for several years now, so she's easily able to contact them.

"Hi, Mr. Cooper? Yeah, it's Kathy. How are you?" There's a pause. "Sorry to bother you so late, but I'm visiting with Lily, and she says she's kind of homesick and would love it if you could pick her up tonight." Another pause. "Yeah, right now, please." Pause. "No, no, nothing is wrong. I think she didn't text you herself because her device is acting up and is not sending texts or something."

If I weren't so upset, I would commend Kathy for her performance.

Before long, my parents are downstairs, waiting for me. Kathy and I head out of the front door, and all the while, I search for Kenny. There's no sight of him, and I wonder if he took off immediately after leaving my room.

"What's wrong, pumpkin? Missing us, eh?" Dad uses the lift to get me in the minivan.

I smile a weak, tired smile, just craving to be in the safety of my own bedroom.

"You look exhausted, honey. Are you doing alright?" Mom asks as soon as she sees me.

"Lily, do you want me to come to your house?" Kathy intervenes, changing the subject.

I quickly nod yes, desperately needing the support of a good friend right now.

When Kathy and I are finally alone in the safety of my own bedroom, I tell her what happened with Kenny.

Shocked, she yells, "That asshole! We are calling the police right now!"

"No!" I yell.

"What do you mean no? He can't get away with this, Lily!"

Calming myself down, I use my device. "I just want to forget about everything. I'm really scared. I don't want anybody to know."

"Are you nuts? What the hell is wrong with you? He hurt you, Lily! You can't give him a pass on that. And, do you know how many other people he's going to hurt if you don't do something about this?"

She's right, of course, but I'm petrified. I have no desire to bring any attention to myself or freak my parents out. Besides, what if the police don't believe me? What if Kenny is right that people won't believe me because they'll think I'm retarded? I hate that word! It's a horrible, horrible word, and it should just be banned from the English dictionary. I've had to deal with this my whole life, always proving my intelligence.

"I don't think I can do it. I'm so ashamed of everything."

"Ashamed? You did nothing wrong! Where's the strong Lily I know? You have exactly ten seconds to find her before I go wake up your parents. This bastard is not going to get away with this. Come on, Lily. You know I'm right on this."

"Nobody will believe me, Kathy."

"Like hell! I'll support you the entire way. We're going to fight, Lily!"

In a way, she reminds me of Layna. Maybe that's why I've been drawn to her from the beginning. Kathy is idealistic and will always fight for the underdogs, just like Layna used to.

Without realizing, my gaze lands on Layna's picture in my room. It's her senior picture, and her wise and strong eyes meet mine. I've never had her strength. As I continue to stare at her, her blue eyes penetrate my soul. I can almost sense the courage rise inside me. Layna would want me to fight. She'd be very disappointed if I hid in a corner. No, those days are gone. Kathy is right. He will hurt other people if I don't do something about it.

"Okay, Kathy. Go get my parents."

"What?" Dad screams. "What are you saying?"

My parents' reactions have upset me all over again. Knowing I can't discuss this any longer, Kathy intervenes. "Luckily, I got there before he could hurt Lily more, but I think we need to call the cops and report this."

Mom kneels next to me and pulls me into her arms. "Oh, Lily. Baby, are you okay? Oh, please tell me what I can do."

"I'm going to kill this bastard! He works for that place? I'm going there right now!"

"No, no, Mr. Cooper. I don't think he works for them directly. I think he must work for an outside agency because he was just filling in for somebody. You won't find him there. He's already gone." Kathy tries to calm him down, but fails.

"I told you not to move out on your own! I told you, Lily! There is evil out there. Horrible people who hurt somebody as helpless as you! Don't you know that?" Dad is still screaming. No longer able to contain his anger, he picks up the kitchen chair and throws it across the room.

All I can do is to stare in horror at the pain I've caused my parents. They both are falling apart, knowing somebody hurt their baby.

"I know everybody is upset right now, but the sooner we call the cops, the better." Kathy again tries to take control of the situation.

"She's right, Bill. We have to call the police," Mom says, finally able to think rationally through her tears.

Dad grabs the phone and makes the call.

Chapter Seventeen

The next few days are a blur. The police take my statements, as well as Kathy's. Kenny is arrested but is soon out on bond. I have a restraining order against him, so he's not allowed to come anywhere near me. The fact that he's out, knowing that I've filed charges against him, scares the hell out of me. For the first time in my life, I'm actually thankful that my parents refuse to allow me to be alone. All three of us have taken leave from work for a couple of weeks, just to try to support and heal.

On the third day away from work, Mark stops by at the house, appearing very distressed. As soon as we're alone, he kneels in front of me, taking my hand. "Lily, I forced Kathy to tell me why you haven't been coming to work. Damn it! As soon as she told me, I headed straight over to see you."

Great! I didn't want anybody to know. "Who else knows?"

"Nobody! Just me, I swear. Look, let's get some fresh air. I'm feeling really claustrophobic, and I really want to talk to you alone, away from here. Can we go walking by the lake?"

Maybe getting out of the house is just what I need. I've been locked up in here for the last three days, afraid to even breathe. Having Mark by my side gives me the courage I've been seeking. The lake is only a few blocks away from the house, so there is no excuse for me to refuse. Once I agree, we both head out.

"It's a good thing Kathy stopped by there when she did. Did she ever tell you why she came?" he asks. I've completely forgotten to ask her about it. When I shake my head no, Mark continues. "Well, I guess you can use some good news right now, Lily. You're going to get a promotion. I hear since you'll be receiving your master's degree soon, they're going to be promoting you to the same level as a teacher. No more teacher's assistant! Congratulations, Lily!"

I want to be happy because I've worked my butt off for all this, but the recent developments have torn me apart. I can't seem to get past the horrible visions and nightmares that haunt me day and night.

Once we reach the lake, Mark sits on the bench, staring off into the distance. "I have something else to tell you, Lily. When Kathy told me what happened, it really upset me. The thought of somebody doing that to you..." Mark shudders.

I don't want to talk about this right now. Why is he bringing this up, knowing I'd want to just forget about it?

"Did he hurt you, Lily? I mean did he rape you?"

"No!" I yell with my own voice. Maybe I shouldn't have come here. Maybe this is too soon, and I'm just not ready for company yet.

"I'm sorry, okay? I had to know. Look, this has really made me think things through." Mark takes my hand and lifts my chin up so I look at him. "I've grown really fond of you through the years, Lily. Surely, you must know that. I care about you...no, probably more than just care about you. You're amazing and beautiful. I find myself thinking about you all the time. I admire you for all you've done and your courage. Lily, I don't want to be just friends. I want more from you. This incident that happened finally gave me the courage to confess how I feel about you."

Shocked, I simply stare at him, finding it impossible to respond. With no warning, Mark leans toward me and brings his lips to mine. Closing my eyes, I allow Mark to take the horrible memories of Kenny away with his soft, tender kisses. The only other time I've been kissed lovingly was when Chance had kissed me, thinking I was asleep. Whereas Chance's kiss was brief, Mark's kiss lingers, and it almost feels strange.

Taking a deep breath, I force myself to relax and try to enjoy the kiss—if for nothing else than at least to shadow the horrendous memories from the attack. Just when I begin to loosen up, Mark is suddenly pulled off of me.

"What the hell! Get away from her!"

I almost faint when I see Chance standing there, holding Mark off of me. Fury like no other fills his eyes as he shoves Mark away from me.

I find myself at a loss for words, watching in disbelief at the events that are unfolding before my eyes.

"Are you going to answer me? Who the hell are you?" Chance

then turns toward me. "Are you okay, Lily?"

"I'm Mark, Lily's friend!" Mark fixes his shirt, which is now unruly from Chance's assault.

"Lily's friend? Really? Lily doesn't go around kissing her friends!" Chance yells. "I'm Chance, by the way. Lily and I are friends. We have a history together."

Mark chuckles under his breath. "Oh, so you're Chance. You're the guy who left her."

Chance spins his head toward me. "You told him about us?"

"Lily tells me everything," Mark says, smiling smugly.

Well, that's not true. I definitely don't tell him everything. As a matter of fact, the only thing I've told him about Chance is that we were good friends at one time and then he left for medical school.

Chance walks up to Mark and looks at him dead in the eyes. Since Chance is considerably taller than Mark, he towers over him.

"Is that so?" he says, clenching his jaw.

Mark doesn't back down. "Yes, Lily and I are close."

Switching his attention on me, Chance says, "Look, I want to talk to you, Lily…alone." Chance then turns to Mark. "Can you give us some space?"

"I'm not going anywhere unless that's what Lily wants," Mark answers, folding his arms in front of his chest.

Both men turn toward me to respond. All I can do is stare at Chance and soak it all in. He has cut his hair shorter now and he is definitely bigger somehow. It looks like he's been working out at the gym with the way his muscles have filled out.

Realizing that they're both waiting for me to answer, I finally think rationally enough to use my device. "It's okay, Mark. I'll be fine with Chance."

Mark walks toward me and grabs my hand. "Are you sure you want to be alone with the crazy guy, Lily?"

I quickly hide my grin when I notice Chance's hands ball up into fists. To somebody as conservative as Mark, Chance probably looks crazy. Mark is used to wearing the button down shirts with dress pants. His hair is always nicely groomed and his face is perfectly shaved.

Chance is his exact opposite. With his fitted t-shirt and his faded blue jeans, Chance watches our exchange like a hawk. Unlike Mark, Chance's hair is disheveled from the wind, and he has a five o'clock shadow from not shaving. I'm sure the fact that he has his earrings on doesn't help his case.

I nod at Mark and after hesitating a few more seconds, he quickly kisses my cheek and walks back to his car.

"Why are you letting him touch you like that?" Chance demands.

Angry at his behavior, I start using my device frantically, telling him exactly how I feel. "Are you serious? I haven't seen you in over three years! How are you just going to show up and act like you have any rights to my life? What are you doing here? And why didn't you tell me you were coming?"

"I'm here because I wanted to see you. I needed to talk to you. And, why would I try to contact you to tell you anything? If I remember correctly, you stopped returning my texts. I kept texting over and over, and you refused to answer me. So don't turn this around on me." Chance is breathing heavily, trying hard to calm himself down.

"You still don't have any right to ask about my life."

"I don't like him. I can't believe you let him kiss you like that!" Chance paces in front of me, opening and closing his fists.

"Not your business!" I wish I can make my device yell and it can convey the emotions I'm feeling right now.

"How do you think I feel? I finally see you after all these years, and you're kissing that loser!"

"That loser is a very prestigious professor at the university."

"I don't give a shit!" Chance yells.

Confused and angry at his behavior, I quickly turn my wheelchair and head toward the house. I have no idea what Chance is doing here, but seeing him brings back all of the feelings I've safely tucked away for a long time. Knowing I need my space from him, I increase the speed of my wheelchair.

Seeing me leave, he runs up to me and steps in front of the wheelchair. "Lily, wait," he pleads. "I'm sorry for being such an ass."

Without saying a word, I steer the wheelchair around him and continue toward my house, desperate for the distance.

As predicted, an hour later, there's a soft knock on my bedroom door and Chance walks in. Ignoring him, I continue to watch the television. I have no idea what show is on, but I need to distract my mind from thinking about the recent events.

Chance sits on the bed and simply stares at me for a few moments.

I pretend to not notice him, making it clear that I'm still very angry.

"You're even more beautiful, Lily. You've grown up," he says, his voice soft. When I don't respond, he continues, "I'm sorry again for my behavior earlier. I lost it when I saw that guy. I'm here because your parents told me what happened with you."

I swing my head toward him, shocked that my parents would share such a private incident with him.

"Lily, when you stopped returning my texts, I still kept in touch with your parents. I called them every week to see how you were doing. I couldn't help it. I had to make sure you were alright. When I called this week—this morning, to be specific—they told me what happened. I jumped on the first flight to come see you. I had to talk to you, to check on you. The thought of anybody doing that to you..." Chance's voice trails off, and I notice his eyes glistening with unshed tears.

I don't want his tears! I don't need anybody to feel sorry for me, most of all Chance.

"Stop!" I yell, using my own voice.

Chance knows immediately what I'm saying. "Lily, I don't know what to say. I keep saying the wrong things, and here I go upsetting you again!" Chance rolls his fingers through his hair in frustration.

I don't know what I want from him either. I just know that I'm upset and angry, and maybe I just need to be left alone. "Please leave now." This time, I use my device.

Chance stands up and towers over me. "No! No, I won't leave. I don't care how angry you are with me, but I'm not leaving, Lily. I won't let you push me away just because you don't want to deal with me."

I swing my arm to shove him. I swing my other arm, furiously wanting to hurt him. Chance grabs my arms and pulls me out of my wheelchair. I yell and scream, not wanting him to touch me. Chance continues to ignore my rage and holds me tightly in his embrace. Hitting him over and over with all my might, I continue to take my fury out on him.

Chance takes the blows, and then lies me down on the bed, landing next to me.

Still having the irrational urge to hurt him, I lash my body around. Without saying a word, Chance holds me down, making sure I don't hurt myself. Unable to control my emotions, the tears that I've been holding back finally flood down my cheeks. I sob in his arms for so many reasons. I cry that I've been violated in the worst way. I cry that it has taken this long for Chance to come see me. I cry that I haven't been able to turn to him for help. And, I cry because he forces me to feel again.

Gentle lips land on my face as he kisses my tears away. "Let it out, Lily. I'm here for you," he whispers.

When my sobs quiet down to occasional hiccups, Chance holds my face with both hands. Looking deep into my eyes, he shows me all of his emotions. I see the pain, the sorrow, the admiration, the respect, and the love. Slowly his lips find mine and he softly teases. Captivated in his spell, I sink against his body, savoring this moment. Chance's kiss deepens, his lips no longer gentle. Panting to catch my breath, sensations that have been deeply buried suddenly awaken.

But in the next instant, Chance pushes himself off of me. "Shit! Sorry, Lily." He takes deep breaths to find his bearings. "That was uncool. I lost control."

I try to shake my head to let him know it's okay, but he's already rolling off the bed.

"It's late, Lily. I'm going to leave this room now before I do something I'll regret. Your parents said I can crash in the spare room while I'm here. I hope you don't mind. We need to talk, though—catch up. There's just so much...let's start over tomorrow. Do you want to stay in bed or get back up in your wheelchair? I can tell your mom that you're ready for bed if you'd like."

How the hell is he so calm and collected when I can barely catch my breath? All I can manage is a brief nod, and he quickly disappears.

Chapter Eighteen

The next day, Chance takes me to the outdoor café in the city since it's a beautiful day. I've been to the place plenty of times with Kathy, and I enjoy the atmosphere. Since I've grown accustomed to eating out at restaurants, it no longer bothers me that I'm out in public and somebody has to feed me. I've learned that ignorant people will stare no matter what, and I'm not trying to prove anything to anybody, especially strangers.

Not very hungry, I order light. Chance assists me with feeding the lemon pound cake as well as the iced coffee. While we're eating, he says, "I'm really ashamed of my behavior last night, Lily. I honestly have no excuse for it."

I hate that he's apologizing. I'm not sorry about what happened last night at all. I remain silent as he continues.

"I want to start over. I've missed you, Lily…a lot."

"You knew where to find me." This time, I can't stay quiet.

"Yes, yes I did. But, you knew where to find me as well. Not once did you try to contact me even though my last message said that I'll assume you don't want to keep in touch if you don't text me."

I look away because he's right. It hurt too much to keep in touch with him.

"So, I convinced myself that's what you wanted. Was I wrong?"

I shrug my shoulders, still avoiding eye contact.

Chance sighs and says, "That's what I thought. But, I couldn't just walk away. So, I respected your wishes and kept in touch with your parents. I called them every week, sometimes a couple of times a week, just to see how you were doing. I'm sure they were sick of my calls all those years." Chance laughs. "But I didn't care. I figured if they didn't want to talk to me, they wouldn't have picked up the calls. Hey, they must really like me because they didn't bust into your room last night when you were screaming bloody murder while beating the hell out of me."

Chance seals his lips tight, trying hard not to burst out laughing.

I can't hide my smile because he's right. I'm sure they heard me screaming and making all sorts of noises. "I guess they know the difference between my screams out of anger versus out of fear," I answer with my device.

"Yeah, lucky for me, I suppose. Wouldn't want to deal with your dad's fury, especially if he has a temper like his daughter's..." Chance is back to himself again, teasing me while watching me blush.

"You deserved it!"

"Hey! You have a mean left hook! I have bruises to prove it."

By now, I can't contain my laughter. Damn, I've missed laughing with him.

"Now, that's better. I've been missing that sound." Chance smiles and reaches for my hand. "I'm not going to lie. I'm glad you got all your shit out. You've always had the habit of keeping your emotions bottled up inside you. I'll take a beating from you any day if it's therapeutic." Chance winks.

I roll my eyes but smile. How does he have the power of stepping back into my life after all these years and making me feel like nothing has changed?

"I love to see you smile because you smile with your eyes." Chance brings his hand to my mouth and rolls his thumb on my bottom lip.

His touch brings back the memories from the previous night, and my lips quiver. Noticing, he immediately pulls his hand away.

After an awkward silence, he says, "I'm done with medical school in two months. I graduate, Lily."

"I know." Of course, I know. Whether I like it or not, he's always been in the back of my mind. "What's next?"

"Residency," he simply states.

"Congratulations. I know you've worked hard." I wait a few seconds before asking my next question. "How have you been feeling? And don't bother trying to hide anything."

"Yes, ma'am! But, I'm happy to report that I've been healthy as a horse. I regularly see the specialist who has been monitoring me for ALS. So far, so good."

I release a sigh of relief.

"Let's talk about you, Lily. You're almost done with your Master's, right? Dang, that's so amazing! How's your job going?"

"Great! I feel like I'm making a difference—you know, one person at a time."

"I know you may not believe me, Lily, but I'm the luckiest bastard around to have met somebody like you. You never cease to amaze me." Before I can respond, he says, "You ready to get out of here? I'd love to go for our long walks again if you're good with that?" When I nod, he continues, "Okay, let me go and pay this bill real quick. Wait for me here. I'll be right back."

I nod again, and he disappears inside. My thoughts linger on Chance. Whether I like it or not, my feelings for him are just as strong. I don't know what last night was about, but we both have purposefully avoided discussing it.

"Finally got you alone." A familiar voice sends chills up and down my spine.

I spin my head to find Kenny standing next to me. Just when I'm about to scream, I feel something sharp in the back of my neck.

"Don't you try it, bitch. I'll end your life with this knife." With a smile on his face, he keeps his voice soft enough that nobody else can hear him. He plays with my hair as if we're on familiar terms. "I told you not to tell anybody, but you didn't listen. You're going to regret this. I should have just fucked you over and over until you screamed for mercy. You're going to take me to court? Nobody is going to believe a retarded person in a wheelchair! You're going to lose and then I'll be free to come after you again." Kenny's sinister laugh echoes in my ear. "So here's how it's going to work. I want you to tell them that everything was a lie. You made the whole shit up and I never did anything to you. If you do, I'll leave you alone. If you don't drop everything, I'll hurt you and everybody in your life. I already know that your friend, Kathy, lives alone. Oh, and I also know where your parents live."

I don't dare move. Seeing him again has petrified me. My chest squeezes tight, and I can't seem to breathe. Every single muscle in my body has tightened from my heightened emotions.

"What the hell is going on?" Chance's voice interrupts the tense moment. As soon as he sees the fear in my eyes, he freezes, immediately sensing something is very wrong.

"Oh, hello! You must be the boyfriend." Kenny moves his

hand away from my neck and reaches for his back pocket, which makes me think that he's hiding the knife from Chance.

"Who the hell are you? Get away from her!" Chance moves closer to us.

"So you're a freak, huh? You're into retarded and handicapped girls? Hey, man, if that's your thing, that's cool. I'll admit, she's hot." Kenny smiles as he places his hand on my shoulder and squeezes it.

Before anybody can respond, Chance dives forward and tackles him. As he straddles Kenny, he delivers one punch after another, creating a bloody mess right there on the sidewalk. Several bystanders grab hold of Chance and try to pull him off, but Chance's rage is relentless.

As the horror unfolds before my eyes, I'm terrified that Kenny will hurt Chance with the knife. Feeling completely helpless, all I can do is scream, "Stop!" But, of course, nobody understands the words coming out of my mouth. It just sounds like I'm screaming senselessly.

Eventually, when Chance is finally pulled off of him, Kenny stumbles back up to his feet. With the crowd now gathered around us, he wipes his bloody mouth and says, "You'll regret this. Oh, and your girl may deny it all she wants, but she loved every minute of it."

Realization comes crashing down on Chance, and he somehow tugs free from the hold on him.

"You bastard! I'm going to make you pay!" Once again, Chance takes Kenny down, swinging wildly. This time, it takes several more people to tackle Chance away.

Somebody must have called the police because my mind registers the distant sirens becoming louder. Kenny must have figured it out as well since he tries to stagger away.

"Don't let him get away!" Chance yells. "He's trying to hurt my friend!"

As soon as Chance says this, the crowd gathers around Kenny, trying to contain him until the police arrive. In panic, Kenny pulls his knife out, pointing it at the crowd. I watch helplessly, praying nobody gets hurt.

Before things go completely out of control, the police reach the scene. As soon as they point their guns at him and demand that he drops the knife, Kenny obliges and surrenders by putting his hands up. Soon, the police have him down on the ground, restraining him with handcuffs.

Chance pulls himself away and rushes toward me. "Lily, are you okay? Oh my god, I shouldn't have left you alone. I'm so sorry." Holding my face with both of his hands, he searches intensely into my eyes for some type of reassurance.

With my eyes wide with fear, I nod and reach to touch his face. Chance grabs my hand and brings it to his cheek, kissing it.

By now, the police approach us for questioning. After Chance explains what happened, I tell them my version with my device. I then notify them that I have the whole thing recorded. Somehow, through the terror, I've managed to maintain some of my wit and activate my device to record the incident. I'm confident that at the very least, the voices can be heard.

"Lily, are you serious? You're a genius!" Chance grabs my face and kisses me on my lips, right there in front of the cops and the bystanders. Somebody starts clapping from the crowd, and the rest of them follow. Soon, everybody there is whistling, clapping, or cheering.

Human nature is interesting. Even through all of the chaos, it craves for something good...something that brings hope.

When Chance finally pulls away, the police request that we follow them to the station, wanting to download everything recorded by my device.

"Are you up for that, Lily?" Chance asks.

No, of course not! I just want to go home and put this nightmare behind me. But, I refuse to give up now. I will not allow this evil bastard to terrorize me and be afraid to stand up for myself. Nodding to Chance, I drive my wheelchair to our minivan.

After lifting me up to the passenger seat, Chance holds me a little longer. "I could have killed him for what he did to you, Lily. I would have if they didn't stop me."

I reach for his face and say, "I know," which sounds like, "Ah oh." But Chance knows me so well that he understands exactly what I'm saying. After a quick peck on my lips and loading my wheelchair, he drives to the station.

Standing Tall

All Grown Up

Chapter Nineteen

Once Kenny finds out about all the evidence against him—especially his recorded confession and threats—he pleads guilty. Apparently, the police have been building a case against him, and they've found more victims willing to testify against him. Finally locked up, I'm assured that he will be behind bars for a long time.

Chance stays a few more days before heading back to school. He takes me to visit Layna, attends my aqua therapy sessions, and performs the massages and stretches with me every night. It's as if nothing has changed between us, and yet, in my heart, I know everything has changed. But neither of us brings the future up, not willing to ruin our time together.

The night before he leaves, Chance asks, "So what's up with you and what's his name?"

I know whom he's referring to, but I act naïve and ask, "Who?"

"That guy from your job. You know, 'the prestigious professor,'" Chance answers as he glares at me while sitting in the chair next to my bed.

I smile. "He's a friend."

Chance stands up from the chair and approaches me. "A friend? Friends don't kiss like that, Lily. What the hell! Do you have feelings for him?"

"We're good friends. Of course, I care for him."

Chance folds his arms across his chest. "Are you guys involved?"

"Involved?" I ask innocently.

"Stop. You know exactly what I mean. Stop playing with me."

"Are you involved with anybody?" I ask, now ready to confront him. Two can play this game. I've seen plenty of pictures of girls throwing themselves all over him.

"What? Why would you ask me that?" he asks, walking away.

"You didn't answer the question."

"No, Lily. I have nothing serious going on with anybody. How can you ask me that?" he repeats.

"Pictures don't lie, Chance," I respond. When he looks surprised, I continue, "Yeah, I have Facebook, too, and I saw plenty of pictures of you and girls all over you."

"They're nobody to me." Chance puts his hands in his pockets, shrugging his shoulders.

"It didn't look like that." I shudder, remembering the picture of the brunette girl kissing him.

"This is ridiculous. I see you haven't answered about Mark. I don't like you with him. I know I don't have any right to make such demands but…well, that's just the way I feel."

No, he doesn't have any rights to my life. Our circumstances have led us to two different paths, and it's something we'll both have to accept.

"Are you going to keep in touch with me this time?" Chance interrupts my thoughts.

I think about that question. Do I want us to keep in touch? The fact of the matter is that he's leaving again. He's got his own life there, and God knows when I'll see him next. Keeping in touch would only cause more pain—probably to both of us.

"No, I don't think we should keep in touch," I finally answer. It kills me to say those words, but I know it's for the best. It hurts like hell to let him go, but I know it'll hurt more to hold on. His happiness matters, and Chance has to find his own path to his happiness.

"Are you serious? Why not, Lily? Please help me understand. I don't want you out of my life. I hate not being able to talk to you every day."

"We're both going to be very busy. It's silly to keep in touch when we both have our own lives to live."

Chance sits on my bed, hiding his face in his hands. After taking a couple of minutes to gather himself, he stands back up and approaches my wheelchair. "Come on, let's do your exercises now." He's ready to change the subject and, truth be told, there's nothing further to discuss on the matter. We both realize that we must live with the consequences of our decisions.

After assisting me to bed, Chance performs his magic on my muscles. He knows my body so well that he can put the right amount of pressure while massaging, and my muscles respond instantly to his touch. After he's satisfied with his work, he lies next to me, pulling me into his arms like he has been doing every night since he's been back.

While playing with my hair, he says, "Okay, I'll come clean. There were a few girls in medical school that I was involved with. But, it was nothing serious—at least not from my end."

Although in my heart I've already known that he's been dating around, hearing him say the words out loud cuts like a knife. I swallow and close my eyes, wishing the pain would pass quickly. Imagining him sharing intimate moments with other girls kills me. At that moment, not only does it feel like my heart is broken, but so is every inch of the rest of my body. I bite my bottom lip, hoping the tears won't sneak out of my eyes.

"None of the other girls have touched my soul like you, Lily," Chance whispers in my ear as he snuggles closer to me.

There's nothing to say. I bury myself into his embrace, savoring this moment before I have to let him go again.

When Chance leaves, there are no goodbyes. He simply disappears the next morning without even coming to see me. I'm not surprised. Chance hates putting himself in situations that are uncomfortable. He'd rather avoid them and run.

Taking a deep breath, I know I must try to pick up the pieces of my life again. I have avoided Mark this whole week, but I need to talk to him. When I ask him to stop by, he comes right over that very same day.

"I heard that guy is locked up now. I was happy to hear that," he says as he kisses my cheek.

"Thank you. Mark, I have to tell you something. I care about you too much to not be honest." I don't want to beat around the bush, but I pause and wait for Mark to respond. When he remains silent, I continue, "I can't give you more than friendship. I'm sorry."

After a few more moments of silence, he takes a deep breath

and says, "It's because of that guy, Chance, right?" When I don't answer, he continues, "I'm not surprised. I saw the way you looked at him. It's obvious you're in love with him."

I look away, embarrassed that he has figured it out so easily.

"He's not reliable, Lily. I hope you know that he'll only end up hurting you."

I don't answer, nor do I share that Chance is already gone, out of my life once again.

"I still consider you a good friend, so if you need anything, don't hesitate to contact me." Mark swiftly stands back up, kisses my cheek, and leaves without turning back.

After our "talk," Mark maintains our interactions at a professional level. Although I miss his friendship, I know this is for the best.

Although a heavy burden has been lifted once I confront Mark, I know I still have to face one more challenge. While my parents and I are watching TV in the living room one evening, I say, "I'm planning on moving out again."

Immediately, I get their undivided attention. "I'm sorry, honey?" Mom asks, but I know she's trying to buy some time.

"I've researched some apartments that may suit my needs. Besides, I make enough money to hire my own personal helpers now."

"Have you lost your mind?" Dad can't stay quiet any longer, but I've been expecting this. "What are you even thinking? After what just happened...Lily, I forbid it!"

"I'm sorry you feel that way. That weirdo is locked up now, and I can't live in fear. I won't do it. I'm twenty-six years old and shouldn't be living with my parents. You know that I can live on my own."

"Lily, are you listening to yourself? There are horrible people out there! You, of all people, should know that! At least with us, you're safe. No, absolutely not! I should have put my foot down the last time." Dad continues to yell, clearly frustrated.

"Honey, can we please listen to her? Please, don't yell." Mom tries to calm Dad down. Turning toward me, she says, "Lily, you do know why we're shocked and concerned about this, right? I mean, I hope you realize that we're both against this decision. Please understand that it's only because we love you and worry about you."

"I know that, but again, this is something I have to do. I have to face the world—the good and the bad. Of course, I'm scared, but I have to conquer my fears. I can't live my life like this forever. Please understand where I'm coming from."

They both remain silent for a brief moment. Finally, Dad says, "Lily, I can't talk about this right now. It's just too much. Can you give me some time to process all this?"

"Yes, because I would love for you to be involved with picking my apartment and interviewing the personal helpers with me." I smile, knowing I'm going to win this battle.

After staring at me like I've lost my mind, Dad leaves the house, slamming the front door on his way out. Mom throws her hands in the air and stomps into the kitchen.

I smile smugly because I know that even if they don't like my news, they understand.

Chapter Twenty

My new place looks like a high-rise building. They have some units that are specifically made for individuals like me. It's a beautiful one-bedroom, one-bathroom apartment and completely handicapped accessible. The doors are wide enough for my power wheelchair to fit, and the shower is a wide walk-in shower so my shower chair can roll right in. The apartment itself is on the eleventh floor, but there's an elevator I can use.

In terms of safety, there's always a doorman downstairs by the front door. He has a company cell phone, so if I should need something, I can just text that number. If, for some strange reason, I may need help in the middle of the night, I can use a switch that's attached to my bed. It's about ten centimeters in diameter, so it's large enough that I can easily activate it with my hand. This switch is connected to the phone that will immediately call the doorman downstairs. The doormen are instructed to call my parents and 911 immediately if they receive a call from me in the middle of the night. I once again thank my lucky stars that I have the assistive technology background and access to the resources.

My parents also buy me the personal emergency activating bracelet which would immediately call the emergency department through my phone. Luckily, all I have to do is turn my wrist a certain way and just bang the switch on a hard surface to activate it.

My parents sit through each interview for every single applicant for my personal helpers. Lauren is still able to help out, but because she now has kids, most of the help she can provide is on weekends. Lauren refers me to some of her colleagues, though, and since I trust her, this works out well for me. It's tricky because many of the applicants are used to helping elderlies and may not necessarily understand how to help somebody like me. So, I decide to put a training manual together, which outlines every single aspect of my care. This includes how to use my power wheelchair and my communication device, as well as how to assist me with feeding, bathing, toileting, dressing, and transferring me. I also list the times indicating exactly when I wake up, go to bed, shower, eat, and toilet. My body has been trained to the routine for years. I don't know why I haven't thought about putting a manual like this together from the beginning. So many times, my caregivers have struggled in the past. The very first sentence reads, "I am an adult with the same intelligence as you. If you can't remember that, then you can't work for me."

Even with all of the precautions, my parents visit me several times a week. Besides their visits, Kathy and I usually hang out together on weekends. This suits me fine because work and living on my own keep me plenty busy to keep my mind occupied. If I allow myself any downtime, then my thoughts immediately drift to Chance. We haven't contacted one another since he left, which is for the best. He's got his goals, and he definitely doesn't need me to slow them down. Yet, a part of me wonders if he's still keeping in touch with my parents.

I may be able to control my thoughts during the day by staying busy, but I fail miserably at night. My nights are haunted by dreams of the familiar touch, the strong arms holding me in an embrace, and those soft lips that awakened the desires I've worked so hard to bury through the years.

ᘒᗡᓀᓀ

I receive my Master's sooner than anticipated, and I'm immediately promoted. I have my own classes that I teach instead of simply assisting other teachers or professors. I preprogram my material into my communication device, so the lectures move smoothly. I also have all of my information not only projected on the screen during the lectures, but it's also available online. Luckily, the classes I teach are focused on special needs and assistive technology. Occasionally, I'm also a guest speaker for other classes.

As I'm finishing up my day at work one day, Dr. Chaudry, one of the professors, approaches me. "Miss Cooper, I think it would

ЈÐ

greatly benefit my students if you could be one of my guest speakers in my class on sexuality."

Immediately, my muscles tense. This is definitely not a topic I'm comfortable thinking about, let alone discussing in front of an auditorium full of students.

"I'm not sure how I can help?" I ask.

"I was hoping you could cover sexuality for people with disabilities. I believe this is a topic that is overlooked, and it's so important that people understand."

I gulp and look away. I don't want to do this, but a part of me also knows he's right. So many times, this topic is a taboo, especially when associated with people with disabilities.

"Can I think about it?" I finally ask.

"Of course. Would you be able to let me know tomorrow? I'm making my schedule for the month."

"Sure, no problem," I answer and drive my wheelchair away.

That night, I stay awake, stressing about my decision. I've purposefully avoided thinking about my own needs and desires through the years. I'd gotten pretty good at not facing that part of my life unless Chance was around me. Even when he didn't try, somehow he was able to arouse those sensations.

But, I've promised myself that I won't run from my fears any longer. Maybe doing this lecture will force me to finally deal with my own issues. Hopefully, I can perhaps teach the students that it shouldn't be seen as a taboo.

The next day, I find Dr. Chaudry and tell him that I can be his guest speaker.

"I'm thrilled to hear that, Miss Cooper. Would you be able to do this lecture next week?"

"Of course," I reply, kicking myself for agreeing to do this.

During the week, I bury myself in my research. It's important that I present this lecture just right so the students understand with an open mind.

After I'm satisfied with the material, I program my lecture into my communication device. I want to be thoroughly prepared since there will be over a hundred students attending this lecture.

"Hello, I'm Miss Cooper and I'll be your guest speaker today. I will be covering sexuality and disabilities. Some of you may have seen me driving my wheelchair down the hallways and may have wondered what was wrong with me. Well, I have Cerebral Palsy. There are different types, but the kind I have has affected me physically. So, I have a hard time controlling my muscles." I pause, glancing through the auditorium full of students. "So, let me just ask you, and please be honest with your answers because I'm not easily offended. How many of you would see me down the hall and think that I was pretty?"

I scan the room and almost everybody raises their hand. "Okay, of all the guys who have raised their hands, how many would ask me out on a date? Again, be honest."

Slowly, the hands lower until no hand is left up.

"That's because you're a teacher," somebody blurts out from the back of the room.

"Is that really the reason? What if I were a student here?"

Everybody remains silent.

"There are many types of disabilities in this world, and, unfortunately, when something or someone is different from the 'norm,' human nature is to avoid it. If we don't understand something, then if we ignore it enough, maybe it'll go away."

I smile to myself because I know I have their undivided attention. They are intrigued and they want to learn.

I then bring up different types of disabilities and play a video on various people with disabilities and sexual needs. Luckily, I've been able to purchase it for teaching purposes and download it for this lecture.

"At the very least, I hope this lecture has made you question certain things you haven't thought about. I do hope you don't automatically shut yourself away from somebody in a wheelchair or somebody who may not walk or talk quite the way you're used to. Remember, everybody has needs and desires. I promise you that most people with disabilities do not allow their disabilities to define them. Do yourself a favor and maybe make an effort to get to know somebody who's different than you. You never know…this person may be the one for you."

When the lecture is completed, to my surprise, some of the students stand up and begin applauding. Soon, the whole class follows their lead. I smile but keep myself busy behind my communication device.

As the students exit, many stop to say how much they enjoyed my lecture and that they will be taking the classes I teach in the future. When I finally leave the auditorium, one particular guy walks out with me.

"My name is Jeremy, Miss Cooper. Thanks for sharing your knowledge with us today."

I smile politely, but continue to drive my wheelchair.

"I'm going to have to confess here. I've always thought you were really pretty when I've seen you around. And now, I'm definitely intrigued. Would you like to go out with me sometime?"

I stop my wheelchair and look up at him in surprise. Jeremy's eyes are twinkling as he waits for my answer. He looks to be around twenty years old, and I have to admit, he's a very good-looking guy. Even though I resist, immediately, I'm captivated by his piercing blue eyes.

"I'm flattered. But no, I'm your teacher, remember?" I answer with my device.

"Well, not technically. I mean I'm not enrolled in any of your classes and you were just a guest speaker here. So…" Jeremy smirks, proud of himself.

I can't help but smile at his charm. He's definitely a confident young man, and I'm proud of him for thinking outside the box. "Truly, I'm flattered. Again, no thank you. It's still a teacher-student relationship. Besides, I'm dating somebody right now."

I have no idea what makes me say that lie. I suppose it must have been an easy way out from this awkward situation. Although I carry myself confidently in front of people, truth is, I've never done well with compliments.

"Wow, he's one lucky guy because he's got himself a gem. Hope he treats you well." Jeremy leans forward and quickly kisses my hand. "Farewell, my lady."

I watch him disappear down the hall, satisfied that perhaps my lecture did make a difference.

Chapter Twenty-one

I take the bus back to my apartment that evening. Luckily, I've become very familiar with the transit system that is able to accommodate my wheelchair. Most of the drivers are also accustomed to me by now, and that makes it very nice.

Exhausted from work, I drive my wheelchair straight into the elevator once I reach the apartment complex. I close my eyes, dreaming of crashing into my bed as soon as I go into my apartment. I know it'll have to wait, though, because Mandy, my personal helper, will be here soon to help me with my evening routine. I have to use the bathroom and my stomach is rumbling from hunger.

Luckily, I don't have to use a key or a key card to open my door. The door is sensor activated, and the sensor has been attached to my emergency bracelet. Living like this my entire life, as well as the knowledge from my degree and research, is definitely a huge asset to my creativity.

When the elevator stops on my floor, I drive my wheelchair out and head down the hall. My muscles feel especially tight today. It may be because I've been stressed about the lecture the entire week. Craving for a bathtub to soak myself in, I'm thankful that at least I'll have aqua therapy this weekend. My body desperately needs it.

Once I reach my apartment door, I swipe my sensor on the switch by the door. As soon as the door swings open, it stays open for approximately twenty seconds. This way, it gives me plenty of time to drive my wheelchair into the apartment.

"Hello, Lily."

I almost crash my wheelchair into the wall when I hear Chance's voice behind me. Shaking like a leaf, I somehow manage to drive into my apartment with Chance close behind.

Immediately, a million thoughts attack my brain. What is he doing here? Oh my gosh! I probably look like crap! How did he know where to find me? Is he really here? I wish he had warned me, so I could have gotten myself ready.

Staring at him with my eyes wide, I remain speechless.

"How about, 'Wow, Chance! Great to see you! I've missed you!'" Chance says, his lips trying to hide a smile.

Still, I'm incapable of responding. No matter how hard I try, I can't shake off that he's standing right before my eyes.

"Okay, fine. I'll do the talking." Chance walks around the apartment. "I love your place. It suits you. And, you look fantastic, as always. I've missed you, Lily."

I can already feel my blood pressure rising. Why does he think he can just come and go in and out of my life as he pleases? What infuriates me the most is that every time he shows up—with no warning—he acts like everything is perfectly normal, as if he's never left.

"How did you know to find me here? And why did the doorman let you up?" I furiously use my device to give him a piece of my mind.

"I keep tabs on you, remember? Besides, I've kept in touch with your parents. As far as the doorman goes, again, I have your parents to thank for that." Chance smiles, proud of himself.

If I could pick something up and throw it at him to wipe that stupid smirk off his face, I would. I can feel the heat creeping up to my face from rage. How dare my parents just dictate who goes in and out of my apartment without consulting with me!

I spin my wheelchair away from him, needing the space to think clearly. Just when I get used to my comfortable routine, he shows up again, disrupting everything that I've worked so hard to build. I can't have my heart be shattered again. This time, I don't think it's strong enough to take it. My only solution is to harden it and not give him the power to bring my walls down that I've carefully constructed.

"Lily, please don't do this. Why are you upset?"

Why am I upset? Why am I upset? Because every time you leave, you take a piece of me with you! I can't allow you to take any more of me!

But, those words remain unspoken. I turn toward him again and ask, "What are you doing here?"

Chance takes a deep breath. "Hmm, where do I start?"

Just then, there's a knock at the door. "Hey, Lily! It's me!" Mandy yells from the other side of the door.

"Who's that?" Chance asks.

Ignoring his question, I drive my wheelchair past him and unlock the door with my sensor. Luckily, we've adapted the door so I can use my sensor to unlock it from inside as well.

"Hey, Lily!" Mandy says as she walks in. By now, we've become good enough friends that she's very familiar with me. As soon as Mandy sees Chance standing in the middle of the living room, her mouth drops.

Chance walks right up to her and says, "Hello, I'm Chance, Lily's friend."

Mandy stares at his extended hand and finally shakes it. "Oh, sorry, I'm Mandy, Lily's personal helper. I'll be assisting her this evening."

"Oh, no need. I can help her today," Chance says nonchalantly, waving her away.

"No," I interject. "I don't need your help. Mandy will be staying."

Chance shrugs his shoulders and takes a seat on the sofa. Turning the TV on with the remote, he says, "Okay, suit yourself. I'll just watch TV while I wait. Oh, and you don't mind if I help myself to whatever you've got in the fridge, do you?" Chance walks into the kitchen and inspects the fridge.

Giving up, I head to my bedroom. Since the bedroom is attached to the bathroom, I close the bedroom door once Mandy follows me.

"Oh, my goodness, Lily! He is gorgeous!" Mandy gushes.

I roll my eyes, not at all surprised that Mandy is taken in by him. He has that gift of winning everybody over, especially the female population.

Mandy realizes I'm in no mood to talk about Chance, so she gets busy with our evening ritual. After helping me in the bathroom and then showering me, she asks, "Do you want me to quickly put on some light makeup or do your hair really quick? You know, for your guest." Mandy smiles and then winks.

I shake my head no. I refuse to do anything out of my usual routine just because he's sitting in my apartment. No, I will not give him that power.

Mandy sighs in frustration. "Fine, but just for the record, I don't like it. I think you should wear something especially nice for him and get ready."

I shake my head no and point to my usual pajamas.

"No, Lily! You can't wear those ugly plaid pajamas! Besides, it's only 8 o'clock on a Friday night. I know you're not already calling it a night."

Actually, I am ready to call it a night. I just need to eat something and then I'm done for the day. Nothing that Mandy can say will change my mind.

Defeated, Mandy helps put the pajamas on me. Once I'm seated back in my own wheelchair with my device, I say, "Thank you. Now, it's time for some food and then that bed is calling my name."

Since I have my Meals on Wheels, all Mandy has to do is heat up my food. While she feeds me in the kitchen, Chance continues to watch TV. I notice that he has helped himself to a peanut butter and jelly sandwich and the beer from the fridge.

Once done, Mandy helps me one more time in the bathroom and asks if she should do anything else before leaving.

"No, I'm good. Thanks, Mandy. Have a great night."

Chance stands up while Mandy is leaving and walks her to the door. "It's nice to meet you, Mandy. Take care of yourself."

"Oh, very nice to meet you, Chance," Mandy answers, giggling.

The interaction is sickening. Does he have any idea what kind of effect he has on the opposite sex? Hell, probably even the same sex.

When Chance sits back down on the sofa, he turns to me. "You calling it a night already? I mean, it's not even 9 o'clock yet."

"I'm tired," I reply, keeping my answers short.

"I thought we'd talk for a bit…you know, catch up."

"Talk about what?" I ask, still irritated that he has my emotions in turmoil.

"Who was that guy today at college who asked you out?" Chance suddenly asks, taking me by complete surprise.

"What?" I ask, using my own voice.

"Well, I was there. Every time I come to find you, there's always some guy hitting on you. What the hell!" Chance swigs his beer.

"What were you doing there?" I finally ask with my device, more confused than ever.

"Actually, I've been in town since yesterday. I stopped in at the college today to see everybody again, especially since they're my old colleagues. Okay, that's a lie. It was mostly to see you. On my way to the staff lounge, I ran into Dr. Chaudry. He always knew we were close friends, so he told me you were about to be his guest speaker. Of course, when I found out it was about sexuality, I got curious. So, here's where you may get mad..." Chance starts to laugh while I glare at him. "I snuck into the auditorium because curiosity got the best of me. I wanted to hear what you had to say."

Completely humiliated, all I want is for the ground to open and swallow me. "Not cool," I respond, keeping a straight face.

"Nope, it wasn't. Like I said, curiosity got the best of me. I must say, though, you did a fantastic job. I was very impressed on how you handled the topic. You captured their attention immediately."

I don't respond because I have no idea where he's going with this.

"And then that punk followed you out. Do you even know the guy?"

"He was not a punk," I answer.

"Well, he was a lot younger than you."

"What? I'm not that old!" I answer, furious at what he's implying.

Chance laughs, apparently enjoying himself. "I'm glad you turned him down."

I sigh, frustrated that he's buying time and not answering any of my questions. Sensing my exhaustion, he stands back up. "Okay, come on, I'll help you to bed. Let me stretch you out for a bit. I promise I'll leave you alone afterward."

I want to refuse his offer, but my muscles have been so tight that I know it will feel really good if he works on them. In the end, my body wins out over my mind. I allow him to take me to bed and massage my muscles.

After working with me for good forty-five minutes, he says, "Much better now. Your muscles are becoming tighter. Still attending therapy on weekends?"

I nod, my body melting under his magical touch. The tighter my muscles become, the more the pain. Although my body has gotten used to this, sometimes it can be so painful that I have to remain immobile until it passes.

"Do you want me to stay the night, Lily? I can crash here."

I shake my head no. Once he lies next to me, I know all the walls will come tumbling down.

Chance tucks me in and says, "Okay, but have dinner with me tomorrow. I'm staying at a nearby hotel."

Again, I shake my head no.

"What do you mean no? I want to talk to you...about things. Sorry, you're not allowed to just push me away just because you don't want to deal with it. I'll pick you up tomorrow around seven in the evening. I'm not taking no for an answer."

Chance gives a brief kiss on my forehead before I can reply and walks out of my bedroom. When I hear the apartment door close, I release my breath that I must have been holding.

The rest of the night, I toss and turn, as the images of him refuse to leave my mind.

Chapter Twenty-two

The next day, the anticipation of seeing him that night has my nerves on edge. Once again, I remind myself of the heartaches every time he leaves, and I wonder why I'm putting myself through this. During my entire aqua therapy session, though, I contemplate on what to wear and how I want my hair done.

I'm glad Lauren is my personal helper today because she has known Chance forever, as well as our history. That evening, when she is helping me get ready, we pick out the black dress from my closet. It's a simple sleeveless dress with a scoop neck style, but it flatters my pale skin.

Although I don't want Lauren to fuss too much, she says, "If you're going to go on a date with Chance, then we're going to do it right. I don't think he's ever really seen you get prettied up, has he? Well, we're going to show him tonight."

Now that I think about it, I don't think Chance has ever seen me outside of home, college, or work. Even when we were in Cancun, we never dressed up for anything. This really will be the first time I actually make an effort to "pretty myself up."

Lauren puts on just enough makeup to accentuate my large green eyes, and since my hair is long down my back, she uses the large curling iron to add loose curls.

When she finally permits me to look at myself in the mirror, I'm shocked as I stare at my reflection. The beautiful woman in the mirror looks innocent, yet confident, soft, yet feisty, and sweet, yet sexy. For the first time in my life, I actually feel sexy.

Suddenly, the insecure part of me questions everything. Why did I go out of my way to get ready? Why am I assuming it's a date? It's just dinner, and we've had plenty of dinners together. Am I going to be totally overdressed?

151

Embarrassed, I turn to Lauren, ready to ask her to help me into jeans and a t-shirt. Before I can say anything, though, she says, "I know what you're about to say, but I'm putting my foot down on this. You look absolutely gorgeous, and there's nothing wrong with us women dressing up and feeling fine. It makes us feel good and keeps the men drooling. Now, I don't want to hear any complaining from you!"

I release a deep breath and smile. "Thank you, Lauren."

After a quick hug, we both head downstairs since it's almost seven o'clock. Knowing Chance, he's probably already waiting for me downstairs. As predicted, I notice my parents' van by the front door. In the past, he has always borrowed their minivan, so it only makes sense that he would do the same again.

Chance steps out as soon as he sees us. I'm relieved that he's also dressed up, wearing black slacks, a black, button-down shirt, and a gray tie. Where he normally wears his hair wild and tousled, tonight he has it nicely combed, away from his face.

After giving Lauren a brief hug, he picks me up and places me in the front passenger seat. As he fastens the seat belt on me, he whispers, "You look stunning."

Once the wheelchair is loaded, we drive to his hotel. Normally, Chance is very talkative, but today, he's especially quiet. I sneak a peek at him, and I notice that his face looks tense. He's not his usual, teasing self. Immediately, my heart sinks. Something has to be wrong to cause him to be this quiet.

When we reach the hotel, he lifts me out of the passenger seat and places me in my wheelchair. I notice it's the MGM Grand Hotel, and the elevator takes us to the top floor. Once he opens his room, I catch my breath when I enter the elegant penthouse suite. The place has ceiling-to-floor windows with a spectacular view of the city.

"Beautiful," I say with my device.

"Hmm," he responds, his voice soft. After watching me intently, he says, "Sorry, I didn't cook for you. I ordered room service…I know you like Italian so—"

"It's great. Thank you." I've never felt this awkward with him. He has always been able to tease me enough to make me feel at ease. I know something is on his mind, causing this strange behavior.

"It should be here any minute…err, the food I mean. I planned it accordingly." Chance brushes his hand through his hair nervously.

"Is there something you want to tell me?" I finally ask. I don't want to play games, and it's better if I know before this date even starts. Suddenly, it hits me. Did he bring me here to tell me about another girl? Maybe he flew here just to tell me personally. I can totally see that. He would think he owes me that much. If he has found a girl he wants to settle down with, he would tell me first. Of course! It all makes sense now. I try to swallow the lump that has suddenly formed in my throat. Feeling claustrophobic, I want nothing more than to get out of here.

"Lily, I do want to tell you something, but hey, let's have some wine first, yeah? I think I need a drink." Chance walks to the bar, taking two glasses out and pouring red wine into them. "I hope Merlot is okay."

He's afraid he's going to hurt me. That's why his hand is practically trembling while he's pouring the wine. All this time, I've been fantasizing about our time alone together. I've dressed up for him and have gone out of my way to put this stupid makeup on and do my hair. Damn, I feel like a fool.

When Chance holds the glass of wine to my mouth to help me drink it, I turn my head away. I don't want the stupid wine, and I definitely don't want him to help me drink it. As a matter of fact, this entire charade is a big joke. I don't want to go through the dinner and this pretense.

"I would like you to tell me what's going on now. I can clearly see that something is stressing you out."

Chance sighs. "You know me too well, Lily. Yes, I'm stressed but..."

"I'm a big girl now, Chance. All grown up. I'm sure I can handle whatever you're going to tell me," I lie.

"Believe me, Lily. I know you're all grown up." He sits on the sofa. "I want you to sit next to me here, Lily."

"No, I can't access my communication device. I need it to be able to talk to you." This part is definitely true, but I also use the excuse because I don't want to be in close proximity to him.

Before he can respond, there's a knock at the door. "Room service," says the voice from the other side.

Without saying a word, Chance heads to the door to open it. Once the food is brought in and the server leaves, Chance takes his place on the sofa again.

"I'm totally screwing this up. I had rehearsed over and over how I was going to tell you. But damn it, I'm fucking up." Chance stands back up and starts pacing.

"Let me make this easier for you. You want to tell me that you've met somebody special and you're in love with her. You just didn't know how to tell me for fear of hurting me. But, you don't need to worry about me. We're friends. Period. I'm happy for you. Neither of us owes anything to the other. So, please, stop acting like this." I put on a brave front…for him. I don't want him to feel bad and think he will hurt me. I just need to smile right now, put on my best performance, and when I'm alone later, I'll deal with the pain.

Chance falls to his knees in front of me. Taking my hands in his hands, he looks deep into my eyes. "Lily, Lily, there's so much I want to say. Damn it, you look so gorgeous tonight that I'm really having a hard time focusing here." Chance pauses. Taking a deep breath, he blurts out, "You need to know that I'm moving back here. My residency will start here in Michigan."

Confused, I continue to stare at him. I don't want him in the same town as me while he flaunts around his new woman. It's so much easier when there's no chance of running into him, and I can just go about my life, shutting my feelings away.

"University of Michigan has one of the top neurology programs. It has everything I'm looking for, so it actually works out perfectly," he explains.

I try to pull my hands out of his hold, but his grip tightens.

"I can see that you're not too thrilled about me moving back here," he continues. "But let me just get this off of my chest. I've wanted to tell you things for so long, but I just didn't know how. I guess I'm a big wimp. All of the years I've known you, Lily…damn, so many memories. When you wanted to give up, you would dig deep within yourself to find that light of hope. When you were backed into a corner, you came out swinging. Every fear you've had, you not only faced, but you conquered it. Every time you fell, it would have been easier to just remain lying there. Amazingly, you not only crawled yourself back up, but you also kept moving forward. Lily Cooper, this is why I'm in love with you. I've loved you since the first moment I set my eyes on you. Your beauty and grace blow me away. You inspire me every day, even when we're miles apart."

I remain sitting in my wheelchair, without saying a word, without moving. For the brief moments, there's simply silence as I try to make some sense out of his words. Incapable of stopping the tears that now roll freely down my face, I reach for him with my arms.

Pulling him into my embrace, I whisper, "I love you." Although it doesn't sound perfect, Chance understands my words, holding me tighter.

"Let me be your hero, Lily. Your fairytale prince charming who carries you off into the sunset. For the simple reason that I love you so much it hurts. You may not like it, but the truth is, I want to always protect you...from any harm that may come your way. Not because I think you're helpless. It's because I love you. And, when you truly love somebody, you protect them."

He takes my seat belt off and stands me up, pulling me into his arms. I cling to him, wishing this moment would last forever.

"The first time we danced, it was to that depressing song, *The Lonely*. I want to dance with you again." Chance reaches for the remote and turns his CD player on. The song, *Hero,* by Enrique Iglesias, comes on. "Every time I hear this song, I think of you, Lily."

I close my eyes and lose myself in the lyrics, sinking into his embrace and allowing the music to do its magic. While we dance, Chance caresses my back, plays with my hair, and leaves a trail of soft kisses on my face and neck.

When the song finishes, he helps me to the sofa and kneels in front of me. "Lily, I don't know what's going to happen to me in the future, but I want to spend whatever time I have left in this world making you happy. I've tried to live without you, and I've been miserable. I'm broken without you by my side. Will you have this broken man and make him whole again? Will you marry me, Lily Cooper?" Chance pulls a small, black, velvet box out of his pants' pocket and takes the ring out.

My head spins as I stare at the beautiful halo engagement ring. Is this really happening? With my emotions so high, my muscles lose control. My arms go one way while my legs kick the opposite direction. Seeing that I'm about to lose my sitting balance, Chance steadies me. "Whoa, wild girl! You're all over the place. Should I take that as a yes?"

Using all of my might, I throw myself forward and into his arms. Chance catches me while he laughs and slowly lowers himself to lying on the floor with me on top of him. I stare into those gorgeous hazel eyes I've dreamed of every single night for so many years. He holds my face with both of his hands, staring back into my soul.

"I didn't get a yes yet," he softly whispers as he slips the ring on my finger.

I lower my lips slowly to his and show him exactly how I feel about him. Chance tangles his fingers into my hair and deepens our kiss. This man not only possesses my heart but also my body. Suddenly, I want more…need more.

Chance picks me up and carries me to the bedroom. "To hell with the dinner."

After sharing some passionate kisses, Chance pulls away. "No, Lily. We're waiting until marriage. I've waited this long for you, and I want to do it right."

Although disappointed, a part of me wants to wait, also. I sigh and snuggle closer to him.

"This dress is gorgeous on you, Lily. When I picked you up earlier…well, just seeing you looking so beautiful…I almost lost my nerve. I've been so nervous like this. Do you know I've been planning this move back for a while? I fought my feelings for you for so long. I had so much guilt. I know we've been friends for a long time, but so many times, I fantasized about making love to you. That's when the guilt started. I mean, we were friends and you trusted me. I should be taking care of you, protecting you. But, when I saw your strength, I knew you were so much more than I had ever dreamed. My feelings for you only deepened. I thought maybe it would be easier while I was away at medical school. Lily, no matter how hard I tried, I thought about you every single day, every minute of the day. I tried to stay busy, even tried dating other girls, but you were always there with me. It killed me when you stopped texting me. I couldn't just let go like that. I'm not strong like you, Lily. You must know that." Chance plays with my hair and lifts my chin up to look at him. "I swear, I think I've loved you from the moment I saw you. I denied it to myself and even tried to stay away. But, it was useless. When I finally got the chance to talk to you while you were waiting for your dad to pick you up that stormy day, I knew I had to know the real Lily Cooper. You stole my heart from the beginning. Do you know how much it killed me when I found out what that bastard did to you? I blamed myself. I should have been with you to protect you." Chance begins trembling, as his emotions get the best of him.

Shaking my head no, I kiss his lips again. I realize now that not only did I need the healing from that horrible incident, but so did Chance. The way he's acting, he may never be able to get over that.

"I'm never going to bring that incident up again, Lily. I promise you." Chance sends tender kisses all over my face. "Lily, I have to be sure. You know what you're getting into, right? There's a good possibility that I may be diagnosed with ALS one day. I don't want to be a burden to you, ever...that's another reason I stayed away. As you can see, though, I've failed miserably. One thing you have taught me is that I can't worry about the unknown. I just have to live day by day and make every minute count."

I hug him tighter, drowning in the sea of bliss.

"You know I asked your parents' permission to marry you?"

I look up at him, surprised.

"Yeah, I asked them officially when I returned back. Your mom cried and your dad said, 'What took you so long? It's about time you put your big boy pants on!'"

I laugh because I can totally picture the entire scene. Sighing deeply, I rest my head on Chance's muscular chest. I close my eyes, savoring this moment and hoping this feeling of pure ecstasy will last forever.

⸙

The very next day, Chance and I head to the cemetery. I need to be close to Layna and share my news with her. As soon as we reach there, Chace places me on the ground and sits behind me to support me.

"Layna, I want you to know that I'm going to marry your sister. I can't promise that our life will be perfect, but I can promise that she'll never have to face it alone. I will look out for her until the day I die." Chance then leans forward and kisses my cheek.

I lean my back against him and close my eyes.

Oh, Layna, I so wish you were here. I want to share this so badly with you. I love him, Layna. But, of course, you knew that. He's wonderful, and I know I'll be happy with him. I just wanted to come here and tell you myself. I want you to give us your blessing, Layna. There's just so much I want to be able to share with you. Remember you used to say how we were both going to marry brothers so we could live together even after marriage? And remember, I would think you were nuts? I never thought I'd be getting married, Layna. Somehow, you knew. You just knew. You were the one who always believed. Thank you, my dearest sister. I miss you so much. I love you, Layna.

The plans move quickly after we're engaged. The date is set ten months down the road, and Chance moves into my apartment with me. Although we've always spent a lot of time together in the past, we've never lived together. Chance has no reservations about helping me with my needs, but still, I continue to have my personal helpers come and assist me, especially for bathing and toileting. Chance has never seen me without my clothes, and I can't help but feel that I'd like to keep it that way until after marriage.

Soon, his residency starts, and he buries himself in his work. He can only take a few days off for our honeymoon, so we decide to keep it simple. We plan to rent a small log cabin in the woods up north for some alone time and really get away from the stress of our everyday life.

Since I have ten months before marriage, I plan a surprise for him for a wedding gift. At my therapy session, I tell my physical therapist my plan.

"Lily, you know you haven't walked that kind of distance for almost ten years now. Your muscles are significantly weaker."

"I'm walking down the aisle. Are you going to help me reach that goal?"

Trina sighs and then smiles. "If anybody can do it, I know it will be you. You already walk very well in the pool with a little bit of help. We have to bring that to the land now. That means extra hard work, though. Instead of one-hour sessions on weekends, sometimes we may need to increase them to two hours."

"I'll do whatever I have to do."

Chapter Twenty-three

The next ten months are busy with wedding preparations, work, and my extended therapy sessions. Before long, I am dressed in my wedding dress, sitting in my power wheelchair at the end of the aisle.

Chance is waiting for me patiently, smiling as he sets his eyes on me for the first time in my wedding dress. My dad stands by my side and gives me a gentle squeeze on my shoulder. Right when the music starts, my therapist brings the walker to me and nods at me with pride and encouragement.

Taking a deep breath, I pull myself to standing position with some guidance from Dad and Trina. I position myself in the posterior rolling walker, which drags behind me while my arms are supported in the platforms to stabilize myself. Until I'm positioned just right, I don't dare look at Chance.

When I'm finally ready to take the first step, my eyes find Chance. He stands there in shock, staring intently with a magnitude of emotions flashing through his eyes. Finding the strength, I take the first shaky step. I've been practicing this distance already with this walker, so I know I can do it. My apprehension, though, has me suddenly questioning if I can actually walk the full distance. I really don't feel like falling in my wedding dress while walking down this aisle at my own wedding.

Once again, I take a deep breath and conjure up all the courage from inside me. I've worked hard all this time for this moment. For Chance. I won't quit now. I take another shaky step, but this time, it's a bit steadier. I focus on Chance, who is waiting for me at the end, encouraging me. I draw the strength from him and keep moving my legs forward. I know that Layna is here. I can feel her supporting me, cheering me on. Each step counts. Each step brings me closer to him. To my future with him. And, with each step, I feel stronger. Although my steps are slow and short, they keep moving me forward as I continue to pull my walker behind me.

Everybody is silent. I think they all may be holding their breaths. Dad continues to walk next to me, holding the crook of my arm. His steady grip gives me the reassurance to keep going. I notice the tears flowing down Chance's cheeks when I finally take my place next to him. I want to reach up and wipe them away, but my arms are strapped onto the platforms of the walker. I maintain my eye contact with him and give him a shy smile.

As soon as my dad kisses my cheek and releases me, Chance grabs my face and kisses me right there in front of everybody. The vows are not even exchanged. As a matter of fact, the minister hasn't even begun speaking. Far off in the distance, I hear somebody clapping and soon, all of the wedding guests are applauding and whistling. This snaps us back to reality, and Chance finally releases me. He wipes his tears away, and we both smile.

The minister clears his throat and says, "Are we ready now?"

"I've been ready," Chance says, never releasing his hold of me with his eyes.

Because I can't repeat the vows, I simply say, "Ya," every time the minister asks me if I agree.

Chance unstraps my left hand and holds me steady while slipping the ring on my finger. Since it would be impossible to put his ring on him myself, he guides my hand while I hold his ring. While still assisting me, we both are able to put the wedding band on him.

Finally, I hear the words I've been waiting for: "I now pronounce you husband and wife."

At the reception, my dad and I dance to *Unforgettable* by Nat King Cole. I stay in my wheelchair while he holds my arms and dances around me. At the end of the song, he pulls me out of the wheelchair and into his arms. "I love you, baby girl. Be happy, Lily."

I kiss my dad on the cheek before he places me back in my wheelchair. Next, Chance dances with my mother to *What a*

Wonderful World for the mother-son dance. Chance has become very close to my parents through the years and considers them his own mother and father. After the song finishes, he escorts my mom back to her chair and kisses her hand.

Chance wanted to surprise me for our first dance as husband and wife. He picked the song himself, keeping it a secret from me.

He approaches me and bows dramatically in front of me. "May I have this dance, Mrs. Ryker?"

I smile and give him my arms so he can stand me up. He carries me to the middle of the dance floor and sets me down as the music starts. *Heal* by Tom O'Dell begins to play and instantly, I see Chance's eyes fill with emotions. I know Chance keeps a lot bottled up inside him. He has talked about his past with me only once, and I'm sure he's never repeated that story to anybody else. I put my head on his chest and cling to him.

He holds me tight while swaying to the music, and my body instantly melts against his. I lose myself in the lyrics, in this magical moment. I can feel his every emotion. In that instant, everything disappears. Nothing matters. There are no worries. All of the pain from the past vanishes. All of the worry about the future fades. It's just about this moment in time. It's about Chance and me.

And we heal together.

As soon as we can, we sneak away. Before leaving, I have my mom help me to the bathroom. Usually, if I use the bathroom around nine, I'm good until the morning. She also helps me change out of my wedding dress and into a simple white dress. I know Chance will have to help me with the bathroom situation during our stay there, but it's just something I'll have to get over.

"Baby, you're radiating with beauty. I'm so happy for you," Mom says, her eyes tearing up. "All this time, I've always seen you as my baby, and now, I have to see you as a grown woman." Mom kisses my forehead. "Are you ready for this? You know I love Chance to death. He's your perfect match, but honey, if you're not ready to be intimate with him, you need to tell him that, okay?"

Oh, great! Leave it to Mom to have the "sex talk" right before

I leave for my honeymoon. I roll my eyes and say, "Okay, Ma." We both giggle, and she helps situate me back into my wheelchair.

Chance and I plan on driving straight to the cabin to start our four days of honeymoon. I assume we'll be borrowing my parents' minivan, but Chance surprises me with a brand new minivan with a lift waiting for us.

When I look at him questioningly, he replies, "Well, I can't keep borrowing your parents' van all the time. We needed one for ourselves, anyway. So, I wanted to surprise you."

I smile and give him a kiss when he lifts me up to the passenger seat. He holds me in his arms a little longer and says, "You make a beautiful bride, Mrs. Ryker. You take my breath away." He lowers his mouth to my lips, teasing me with his tender kisses.

During the two-hour drive, my anticipation builds. Suddenly, I'm nervous about being alone with him. Sure, we've been living together and sharing the same bed, but Chance has always backed off before anything further than passionate kisses can occur. I can sense that he's just as nervous as me because the closer we get to our destination, the quieter he becomes.

Finally, when we reach the cabin, it's almost midnight. He picks me up and holds me out in the open country air. We both lose ourselves as we stare at the sky full of stars. They twinkle down on us, smiling with happiness.

After kissing me outside while he cradles me in his arms, he eventually brings me inside to the sofa. As I inspect the beautiful log cabin, Chance heads back out to bring our belongings, including my communication device and my manual wheelchair. We've purposefully decided to bring the manual wheelchair because it will be easier to maneuver.

He helps me into my wheelchair and attaches the communication device on it. "I know it's late, but I want to talk with you for a while, Lily."

I smile, nodding. He's buying us some time and hoping to ease up some of the nervous energy radiating between us.

"How long have you been practicing walking?" he suddenly asks.

"I started working on it soon after we were engaged. I wanted to surprise you," I answer, proud of my accomplishment.

"Surprise? I was shocked! I thought you hadn't been able to walk like that for over ten years now."

"Believe me, I worked my butt off to do that walk down the aisle. It wasn't easy."

Chance takes my hands and kisses them. "When you set your mind to something, Mrs. Lily Ryker, you apparently can do anything. I'm flattered that you worked so hard for me. You know what this means, right?" Chance throws me a mischievous grin. "We're adding the walking as part of our sessions now. As a matter of fact, I brought that walker with us in the minivan."

I can't help but laugh. Why am I not surprised? But, truth be told, I plan on continuing to work hard on keeping the walking skill. I know if I slack off even a little, I'll lose it completely again.

Suddenly serious, Chance says, "Lily, are you nervous about tonight?"

I look down and shrug my shoulders.

"I figured you'd be nervous, but I'm nervous, too. I mean, if you're not ready for it, I totally understand. There's no pressure just because it's our wedding night. I'm a very patient guy. I'll wait for you."

I frown. Has he lost his mind? Just because I'm a little nervous doesn't mean I don't want to do it. I mean, I've waited a long time for this! Besides, I'm well prepared for this moment. I've been on birth control pills for the past few months, and I've made sure that I'm nicely groomed...everywhere. No, he's not getting out of this.

"We're doing the deed tonight, Chance," I reply with my device. "And, I'm looking forward to it."

Chance laughs, his eyes dancing. "Well, okay, then! I'm here to please! But first, do you need to use the bathroom?"

"No, I'm good. I need help with brushing my teeth, that's all."

"Lily, you know you're going to have to get used to me helping you with personal things, right? We've gone through way too much together for you to be shy about it." Chance squeezes my hand.

"I know, but not tonight. Not on our wedding night."

Chance smiles. "Okay, fair enough."

After helping me brush my teeth, he brings me to the bedroom. I gasp when I see the huge king size bed with a canopy, surrounded by sheer white drapes around the pillars. The mattress is covered with rose petals. I have never seen a more beautiful sight.

When I turn to him questioningly, he shrugs his shoulders and says, "Just wanted to show you that I can be romantic at times."

"I love you," I say, using my own voice.

"I love you, my dear wife." He helps me to lie down on the bed. Soon, he turns off the lights and lies next to me. The moonlight trickles into the room, shimmering and dancing.

Chance turns toward me and pulls me into his embrace. Playing with my hair, he says, "Mm, you smell really good." He pauses. "Lily, I'm scared. I don't want to hurt you."

I stiffen up. Here we go again. I'm already nervous enough, and he's not helping the situation. Somebody is going to have to take charge of this situation. I manage to slip my hands under his shirt. Bringing my lips to his mouth, I kiss him deeply, letting him feel my passion, my longing.

It works because soon we're both breathing heavily. Chance catches his breath and says, "I love you, Lily. More than you'll ever know. I want to do this right. I'll try to be as gentle as I possibly can, but the first time for a girl is painful. And, probably not even pleasurable. But, I'll do everything in my power to make it a pleasant experience for you."

True to his word, Chance is gentle and loving. He makes me feel sensations I've never felt before. There are times when I'm holding him for dear life, squirming under his touch, and screaming in pain and pleasure. He brings out a part of me I never realized existed.

But most of all, he makes me feel beautiful.

Chapter Twenty-four

'm sorry, Lily. I hurt you." I hear Chance whispering in my ear the next morning.

Opening my eyes to the sun shining through the window, the memories from last night come flooding back. Suddenly shy, I hide my face in his chest.

"Look at me, Lily. Are you okay?"

I nod. Of course, it hurt, but I also enjoyed it. I touch his face and kiss him to reassure him that I'm doing just fine.

"Okay, you probably need to use the bathroom. I found your nightie this morning. Here, let me help you put it on."

Suddenly horrified that I'm still stark naked, a look of panic flashes in my eyes.

Chance chuckles. "I'm pretty sure I've seen every inch of your body by now, dearest Lily. Still, watching your face blush like that is endearing."

I roll my eyes as he helps me into the Victoria's Secret lingerie. Kathy had insisted on buying me the sexy lingerie, teasing me that I'll need it for my honeymoon.

Once Chance brings me to the bathroom, he helps me sit on the adapted toilet we have attached to the regular toilet.

After securing me properly on it, Chance says, "Okay, I'll give you some privacy. Just holler when you're ready."

As much as I hate the situation I'm in right now, he's right. I just have to get over my hesitations. It is what it is, and it's not like I'll be able to do some of these things by myself miraculously. Chance is now my husband, and he has vowed to stand by my side through all that life has in store for us.

When I'm done, Chance helps to clean me up. He's a natural and not once makes me feel awkward. "Now, that wasn't so bad, was it? Besides, who knows? You may have to wipe my ass in the future."

Leave it to him to make light of our situations. I laugh. And, I laugh some more. Soon, Chance laughs with me. For some reason, we laugh hysterically with Chance sitting on the floor and me still sitting on the toilet. The whole scenario is hilarious. I suppose in awkward situations like this, laughing is so much easier than crying.

"Come on, let's take a bath. I'm ready for the Jacuzzi, how about you?" Chance winks.

I smile at his silliness.

After filling the tub with the water, he brings me to the edge of the tub. While stabilizing me, he pulls the clothes off both of us.

"I know how well your muscles relax in the water. I think you'll enjoy this experience, Mrs. Ryker."

Soon, we're both submerged in the water. He's sitting behind me and my back is leaning against his chest. Closing my eyes, I allow the hot water to do its magic.

Chance kisses my neck, playing with his tongue. As he soaps me down, his fingers linger on my breasts. My breath catches as Chance continues his exploration.

When my muscles tighten up because of the sensations he's creating, he whispers, "Shh, my Lily. Just close your eyes and relax. Enjoy the feeling. Give yourself to the sensation."

I slow my breathing down and sink against him, allowing my muscles to relax. Nothing can stop the soft moans from escaping me, especially when his hands continue their in-depth exploration. I feel myself rising until I have no control left. When my body finally releases, I scream Chance's name.

Chance holds me tightly until I come back down to Earth. Wow, just wow. What the hell!

I've always heard of orgasms, but I've never experienced them. I've just assumed because of my crazy muscles having a mind of their own, I probably couldn't even have such a sensation. Boy, am I glad I've been wrong on that.

Soon, Chance has me lying next to him. He turns me toward him and stretches my leg over his. "It'll be less painful in the water," he whispers.

This time it doesn't hurt as bad as last night. This time, I allow the pure pleasure to consume me. Nothing is more exhilarating than watching Chance fall apart while making love to me.

The honeymoon passes too quickly. Outside of both of us enjoying the country air, exploring nature, doing my exercises, and Chance cooking us homemade meals, we learn each other's body in depth. By the end, I'm even brave enough to do my own exploring to find out what pleases Chance.

By the time we arrive back home, I lose all of my reservations around him. There are no awkward moments between us. If I need help with anything, I ask him. If I don't, he respects me to do it on my own.

Life gets busy fast. I continue to work hard, and Chance buries himself in his residency. Through it all, we still manage to make time for one another and catch up on our day.

Eventually, Chance wants us to move out of the apartment and buy our own home. He says he still has a lot of money left from his parents, and he thinks we should use it for a new home. We buy land and build a completely accessible "smart" house. With my assistive technology background, we try to think of everything we need or may need in the future. We even build an elevator that can take us between the two floors.

My life has changed dramatically, but one thing doesn't change. Every weekend, Chance takes me to visit Layna. There, I tell her my deepest thoughts and fears.

Chance continues to show no signs of ALS. He obsessively throws himself into his research. He still believes that stem cells may be the answer to help many illnesses.

Although Chance seems to have found his purpose through his research, I still feel a void in my life. While watching a movie on the television one evening, I bring up the topic of kids.

"I think we should try having a baby."

Chance nearly chokes on the gulp of beer he has just sipped. "Uh, no. Have you lost your mind?"

"Why not?" I insist.

"We've discussed all this already before marriage, Lily. I can't believe you're actually saying this. No kids. Period. Please don't bring it up again." Chance stands up and goes in the bathroom, slamming the door behind him.

I continue to stare at the television, fighting back the tears.

After his residency, Chance works as a neurologist, treating patients as well as playing a vital role in research. As he becomes fixated on his research, I bury myself even deeper in my work. Although I decrease my hours at the college, I pick up another job. Various agencies hire me as a consultant to evaluate homes of people with special needs and recommend technology to assist them with independent living. My clients completely trust me since they see me living on my own, and if I can make a difference in someone's life by providing them with any type of freedom, then I've already reached my goals for my career.

Even with everything I've accomplished and Chance by my side, there's still a nagging voice inside that reminds me I need more in my life. I desperately want to start a family, but with Chance not willing to listen to my reasoning, it's impossible to even bring that subject up to him. He leaves me no choice but to take matters into my own hands.

Before going up to our bedroom one night, I tell him that I want to talk to him. "There's something that I need to tell you."

"What's up, babe?" Chance sits down on the sofa next to me, giving me his undivided attention.

"Do you ever feel like something is missing in your life?"

"Lily, I have everything. I'm married to the woman I love. I have a great career, and so far, I'm free of ALS. I'm content, actually. Why? Do you feel like something is missing?" Chance reaches for my hand, his eyes full of concern.

"Yes, I do. I know you hate talking about this, but I really think you would make an amazing daddy."

Immediately, Chance pulls his hand away. Standing up, he starts walking away.

"Please, listen to me," I beg. I've already got something programmed into my device, but I need to first make sure that he's ready to hear it.

"Lily, once again, this is just crazy. Please stop. The answer is no. Absolutely not!"

"Well, it's too late!"

Chance spins around to face me. Narrowing his eyes, he says, "What do you mean?"

"We're having a baby, Chance. I'm pregnant."

For a few seconds, Chance doesn't say a word. I think he even stops breathing. Then, very slowly, he says, "Is this some kind of joke, Lily? It's not funny, so stop now."

"No joke. I got tested at the doctor's." Kathy had taken me to the doctor's appointment this morning. I've been suspicious, so I asked her to accompany me.

"That's impossible. You're on the birth control pills." I see Chance clench his jaw, trying to stay calm.

I lift my head up, preparing myself for his rage. "I stopped taking those months ago."

Chance walks to the kitchen and takes a swig of whiskey. When he's ready to continue our conversation, he walks back to me.

"Lily, please, please tell me this is not true." When I remain silent, he says, "How could you? You knew how I felt about it. How could you make a decision like that without discussing it with me first? You deliberately betrayed me."

"I tried to talk to you. Many times! You refused to listen."

"So you're going to just decide this on your own? We're partners in this marriage. You can't make a big decision like that. What the hell!"

"You decided we weren't going to have a baby. Not me! In our past discussions, you never gave me the opportunity to discuss how I felt about it. I never agreed to that decision."

Chance tangles his fingers in his hair, and I think he even pulls it. "Are you listening to yourself? For such an intelligent woman…damn it, Lily! I'm so angry right now!" Chance has lost all control by now and is screaming at the top of his lungs. "I'm sorry you made such a crazy move, but we'll be making an appointment first thing to abort it."

"No!" I scream.

"No? Sorry, but I will not budge. I'm calling one of my colleagues first thing tomorrow morning."

"I'm having this baby." There's no way I will give in to him on this.

Chance pounds his fist into the wall, making me jump in my wheelchair. I stare at the hole his punch creates, holding my breath.

"What the hell is wrong with you? Did you forget that ALS

runs in my family? You want this baby to have that? Is that it? You want the baby to suffer because you're so hung up on having a baby? What if the baby has Cerebral Palsy? And what about you? Can your body even handle the stress of pregnancy?" Chance's entire body shakes with rage as he tries to control his heavy breathing.

"You already know that Cerebral Palsy can't be inherited, Chance." Remaining calm, I take a deep breath and click the icon that already has the preprogrammed message from earlier. "I know you're upset. I'm sorry for hurting you. I'm also sorry that I deceived you like I did. I know it was wrong, and I wish I didn't resort to that. I have deep regrets for betraying your trust. But, I am not sorry about this baby. Every time I've tried to bring this topic up to you, you've pushed me away. I know you're worried about everything, but I can't live like that. I can't think of what ifs. Whatever happens, I'll deal with it. I always have dealt with what life has thrown my way. I understand the consequences of my decision, and I really hope I don't lose you, Chance. I hope that you'll change your mind and will welcome this baby—our baby—into this world. But, if you can't forgive me, I understand. I will have this baby with or without you. Hopefully, the baby will be healthy, but either way, I'll love this baby and I'll teach him or her to be strong. You know I love you to death, but I don't agree with you on this one. I know you like to be in control of life so it goes smoothly. But, it just doesn't work that way. So, you have a decision to make now. If you can't deal with me having this baby, then I guess it's time to say our goodbyes. Like it or not, I will be having this child." Without saying anything further, I turn my wheelchair away from him and head toward the elevator.

"Damn you!" Chance yells as he throws the whiskey bottle across the room. As the sound of the glass shattering echoes in the house, my heart shatters with it. Determined to stay strong, I continue driving my wheelchair without turning around.

As I wait anxiously in our bedroom, I hear the front door slam. I guess Chance is heading out somewhere in the middle of the night. It doesn't surprise me. This is how he has always dealt with things when he feels like he's losing control of the situation. He runs.

Hardening my heart, I wheel myself to the bathroom. I've made the toilet accessible with the rails so I can safely transfer by myself. I try to brush my teeth once I'm back in my wheelchair. I don't know why I even bother. I've tried this a million times but not only can my hand not hold the toothbrush, but I can't even aim it toward my mouth without getting the toothpaste all over my face. Giving up, I transfer myself into the bed.

As I lie there, I relive the entire scenario from earlier. It's already midnight, and Chance is not back yet. I wonder if he really is walking out on me. As the tears sting my eyes, I refuse to cry. Blinking them away, I promise myself that I need to stay strong—if for no other reason than for this baby.

Somehow, I must have dosed off to sleep. When I feel Chance's arms wrap around my waist, I know he's back in bed. I have no idea what time it is, and he reeks of alcohol.

"Lily, Lily. I'm so sorry," he whispers in my ear as he caresses my back. "I'm scared shitless. First of all, I'm scared something bad is going to happen to you. I know people with Cerebral Palsy have kids, but I still can't imagine that type of stress on your body. I can't lose you, Lily. You're my everything. I know I acted crazy earlier, but if something happens to you…no, I won't be able to go on. I try to act strong, but you must know that I'm not. You're so much stronger than me. You've always been able to deal with things. But me? No, I can't do it. And, I'm terrified of the ALS. I'm weak—an ass, really. Lily, I love you. I love you so much it hurts sometimes. You have to know that." Chance continues to say he loves me over and over as he drifts off to sleep.

I Choose Strength

My Life, My Way

Chapter Twenty-five

I don't just get the "morning" sickness. I get the "all day and all night" sickness. Eventually, I need a bucket right next to my bed and one in the car. Soon, I have to take leave from work. Vomiting every hour, even when there's nothing but acid left in my stomach, is the worst feeling in the world.

Chance is beside himself. "You're losing more and more weight. You're supposed to be gaining weight. Lily, this is absolutely nuts."

But I continue to ignore him. No matter what happens, I know I'm not going to quit. I'll find a way to keep going. My baby depends on my strength.

Eventually, Chance asks my parents to move in with us. He feels our house is large enough, and he's not comfortable leaving me at home, even with a caregiver. Since my mom has taken early retirement, she will be available for me if needed.

My parents also believe it's a great idea. They have tried to talk me out of having this baby, saying that my stubbornness is restricting me from thinking rationally.

Believing that all of this nausea and vomiting will stop after the first trimester, I'm extremely disappointed when it continues. Chance insists on attending all of my doctors' appointments with me. He doesn't understand why they can't help me with my nausea. Even the medications they give me don't stay down. A few times, I end up in the emergency room, and they end up giving me intravenous fluids for my dehydration.

Since I'm seeing a high-risk doctor, Dr. Nowak, he monitors me closely. Both Chance and I decide that we don't want to find out the sex of the baby or have any special tests done to find out if there are any defects. By now, Chance has accepted the fact that no matter what the results may show, I plan on giving birth to this baby. It will probably be for the best if he is surprised with the rest of us when the baby arrives. I have to admit, although he is worried sick about me, he has made a one hundred percent transformation with his attitude. He is supportive, and I can even see how he's caught up with emotion every time we watch our baby through the ultrasound.

Unfortunately, my sickness goes from bad to worse. Because of my weakness, I lose more control of my muscles. It becomes even harder to stand, keep my trunk upright, and even swallow. By the time I'm seven months pregnant, I have to be hospitalized. I can't keep anything inside me, and my severe dehydration causes me to start early contractions. At the hospital, they place an NG tube inside of me so the food can travel directly from the tube placed into my nose all the way down to my stomach. The doctors know that they have to get some nutrients and fluids into me.

Dr. Nowak fears that I may have to deliver the baby early, but he promises that he'll try to prolong it as long as he can. I know that the longer this baby can stay inside me the better. It needs to grow some more so it can breathe on its own once born. I want to try to avoid a premature birth for fear of the baby having a higher risk of Cerebral Palsy.

Chance is worried about both of us. He sleeps at the hospital every night. On the nights he's called into work, my mom stays with me.

I can tell my body is completely changing. If I ever want to bounce back from this pregnancy, I'll need to be ready to do some hard work to get my strength back. At this point, I don't even care. Some days, I feel so bad that I truly believe I won't make it. Yet, all I care about is having this baby. I'm obsessed with bringing this precious life into this world. If that's my last hurrah, then I'll die happy.

Of course, I don't share any of this with Chance. Every time he asks me how I'm feeling, I smile and indicate that everything is good. Even if I wanted to share my thoughts with anybody, I wouldn't be able to. I haven't been able to use my communication device for months. I simply don't have the strength, energy, or coordination.

I spend the rest of my pregnancy at the hospital. Absolutely miserable and missing my home, I try to stay positive. I remind myself that soon I'll be able to see my baby. Every night, I dream about what my baby may look like. These dreams continue to provide me with the strength to keep hanging on.

Luckily, I have plenty of visitors at the hospital. Besides everybody from my work, my therapists and personal helpers continue to check on me. Kathy is a regular and even helps to relieve people by staying at the hospital at times. This keeps me busy, and I insist on getting out of bed every day and into my wheelchair no matter how bad I feel. Luckily, the hospital therapists come and see me daily, and Chance diligently massages and stretches my muscles every night.

As much as I try to hold this baby inside me as long as I possibly can, my water breaks at thirty-three weeks. Soon after, my contractions intensify.

Dr. Nowak immediately comes to speak to us. "The good news is the tests show that the baby's lungs are developed. The bad news is this baby needs to come out now because the heart rate keeps dropping. And, I'm afraid you'll need a C-section because the baby is breech."

Although Chance looks like he's about to pass out, I am calm and ready for this moment. I'm not afraid of the C-section. I just want my baby to be brought into this world safely.

"Congratulations! It's a beautiful girl!" Dr. Nowak announces. He quickly wraps her up and places her right on my chest before they whisk her away to check her. I turn my head to stare in awe at this innocent being. Did I really bring her into this world? Did Chance and I truly create her? Nothing can ever replace the emotions that I'm feeling right now. I want to laugh and cry at the same time. My baby girl is, indeed, a beauty.

Chance has been by my side through the entire surgery, but now, he stands by our baby, his expression full of wonder. When my eyes find his, I see that he's just as shaken up as me.

He approaches me and kneels down as he kisses my hand. "She's beautiful, Lily. She has your eyes. She's perfect. You've made me the happiest man alive. Thank you, thank you."

I try to smile at him, but his voice is drifting. I can feel my eyelids becoming heavier. Why can't I focus anymore?

"Mrs. Ryker, close your eyes. I need you to sleep for a while." I hear somebody providing instructions. Who is that? The anesthesiologist?

No, I must stay awake. My baby needs me. I fight it and force my eyes to stay open, turning my head toward our daughter. She's being examined by more doctors and nurses. I must hold her.

Chance must have realized how distressed I am becoming because he stands up and walks to the baby. "Excuse me. My wife would like to hold our baby now."

Without waiting for permission, he picks her up and brings her to me. He places her on my chest again, holding her, and I release my tears of joy. Instinctively, my baby finds my breast and begins to suck. She's perfect. I delivered a perfect baby.

No longer able to fight the anesthesia, Chance says, "Lily, it's alright. You need to rest. I'll make sure our daughter is okay."

I turn my head toward the voice, and Chance's reassuring eyes stare back at me. Okay, he'll make sure she's alright. I can rest now. Watching my precious baby as my eyelids start to close, the darkness finally takes over.

The next time I open my eyes, I'm in the hospital room, surrounded by Chance and my parents. I search for my baby, but panic when I don't see her in the room.

As soon as Chance sees me awake, he rushes toward me. "Lily, how are you? You did awesome! I told you, you're the strongest person I know! And guess what? Our baby takes after you—just as strong. She can breathe on her own and already is looking at everybody." Chance's eyes are beaming with pride as he speaks about his daughter.

I speak to him with my eyes, letting him read my expression.

"They have to keep her in PICU for now. Probably not long, though. You just had surgery so they'll want to clean you up. I promise I'll ask them when I can wheel you over there so you can be with her."

"She's strong like her grandpa!" Dad intervenes. "You did

awesome, Lily. Wait till you see her. She's a beauty."

"She has green eyes like you, Lily. She's so precious. Oh, honey, you've made me the proudest grandma around!" Mom's face is beet red, overcome by emotion.

Now, if only I can hold my baby.

A few hours later, at my insistence, I am sitting in the PICU area with our baby in my lap. I've brought the supporter that cradles the baby and wraps around my neck to help me hold her securely against me while she breastfeeds.

As I watch her innocent mouth sucking, I wonder how she's so perfect. Do all parents think their baby is beautiful? I swear I've never seen anything more gorgeous and precious in my life.

Chance sits next to me while our baby bonds with us. I look up at him, and I notice he's trying hard to hold back the tears. When I lean into him, he plants the most tender and loving kiss on my lips.

"I want to name her after you. She has your eyes and looks just like you," Chance whispers.

As I watch her, she reminds me of Layna. Her gentle features and her graceful movements are a perfect replica of my sister.

"Layna," I say to him. He has heard me say Layna's name hundreds of times, so although I can't pronounce it perfectly, he knows immediately what I'm saying.

He smiles. "Layna it is. You've already given me everything a man could possibly want in life. I love you, Lily Ryker."

Layna Elizabeth Ryker comes home a week later, and she becomes the center of our universe.

Chapter Twenty-six

Our lives change dramatically. Layna has stolen all of our hearts. If she cries, we all try to meet her needs. If she smiles, we all laugh like it's the most precious display ever. Chance can't get enough of her. Watching the two of them interact makes me realize that the best is yet to come.

I don't return to work immediately because I know I have to work hard to get my body and my muscles back to the way they were. I've also lost my ability to walk due to being in the hospital for so long, so that means extra hard work in therapy. Besides getting myself better, I take the leave because I want to be with my daughter. I know that every minute with her is priceless.

I notice that Chance also is less obsessed with his research, now avoiding the long hours at work. He's home more, playing with Layna and helping to take care of her. My parents also officially move in with us, which works out perfectly. Mom helps with Layna and brings her to me whenever I want to hold her or she's ready for her feeding. In the evenings, Chance likes to hold her against me so he can be part of the breastfeeding experience as well.

Although the doctors have monitored Layna closely and said she's healthy, I continue to watch the way she moves. It would kill me to find out that she has Cerebral Palsy. I know it's not genetic, but she is a premature baby and sometimes, that's a risk. To my relief, Layna continues to meet all of her milestones on time and demonstrates normal muscle control and movement.

Once Layna goes to sleep every night, Chance focuses on my exercise sessions. He pushes me more than ever. "You have to work hard if you want to get back everything you lost, Lily. I'm not going to listen to you saying you're tired or you want to rest. I know you can do this, and I'll help you through it. But, you're not quitting."

Easy for him to say. I must have not realized the extent of my weakness from my pregnancy. As much as I want to tell him to go to hell, I know he's right. With him insisting that quitting is not an option, I push myself harder than ever before. I do it for me, for Chance, and for Layna.

When we are in bed one night, Chance starts playing with my hair. "I can tell your muscles are improving, Lily. The tight ones are relaxing more and the weak ones are getting stronger."

I nod, smiling.

"Lily, thank you. Thank you for bringing Layna into our lives. I was a fool. She is truly a gift. A gift you gave me."

I snuggle closer to Chance, closing my eyes.

"We haven't been intimate in a long time. Do you feel like messing around?"

I fling my face up to meet his eyes as they dance mischievously. God, how I miss his teasing. He's right about the "long time." Since I've been sick most of my pregnancy, neither of us has been in the mood to do anything. But damn, I do miss our "intimate" acts.

I play with his chest and kiss his neck to show him my answer. Instantly, I hear him moan. "I've missed you, Lily. I need you so bad. Will you have me?"

When I kiss his lips passionately, there's no turning back.

Chapter Twenty-seven

C hance, Layna, and I create our own heaven on earth for the next fifteen years with my parents standing right by our side. Just when everything is going perfect, though, life always finds a way to throw a curve ball.

On one Saturday afternoon, as I laugh hysterically watching Chance and Layna playing basketball, Chance falls flat on his face suddenly. I gasp because he continues to lie there without moving.

Layna runs to him, yelling, "Dad! Dad, are you okay?"

I drive my wheelchair to check on him, worried sick at why he's not moving. When Layna starts to panic, I notice him moving around, trying to get back up. To my relief, I hear his voice.

"It's okay, Layna. I'm okay. I just tripped, that's all."

Chance remains sitting on the ground, so Layna sits next to him. "Since when have you ever just tripped? You're the one who kicks my butt, even though I'm the one on the high school basketball team," she teases.

Chance laughs, but I can tell it's forced. "Guess your dad is getting old."

Layna laughs with him and tugs his arm to help him stand back on his feet.

When he glances my way, I see the dreaded fear in his eyes.

That week, Chance is officially diagnosed with ALS. The hope that he may not get the disease since he hasn't been showing any symptoms is suddenly shattered. Chance's worst fears come true.

Although devastated, Chance tries to remain upbeat. He follows all protocols from the specialists, but avoids talking about his feelings. I don't know what's worse. Being born this way so never experience "normal" or experiencing "normal" and have it all taken away. This news is not only tearing him apart, but it's also killing me. What does this mean? How fast will it progress? How is he going to be able to handle the changes in his life? How is Layna going to deal with the news? What am I going to do without my strong Chance?

The answers come quickly. Unfortunately, once Chance is diagnosed, the disease progresses fast. His muscles fatigue easily, and there are times when he can't even turn a door knob to open the door. I watch him silently as it takes a toll on him mentally. I try to be there for him and hold him tightly at night, hoping to transfer some of my strength into him.

Chance continues to work as much as he can, but soon he has to decrease his hours. His body simply can't handle the long hours. Although I've been working full time ever since Layna started school, I now decide to decrease my hours as well. I need to be home with him. I can see that depression is hitting him hard. Yet, he refuses to talk about it.

When we're by our lake one evening, I notice Chance walking very slowly and needing to sit down and rest at every bench. Layna is now sixteen years old and walking ahead with her friend, Ryan. I have a feeling they're interested in one another, but Chance is not doing well with her possibly having a boyfriend. He won't allow her to be alone with the boy, even if it's only an innocent walk. So, here we are, chaperoning them. Unfortunately, Chance is having a hard time keeping up.

"I know you don't want to hear this, but maybe you need a wheelchair for long distances," I say with my device.

Chance doesn't look at me, but continues to watch his daughter as she walks with Ryan. Taking a deep breath, he says, "I can't have her watch her strong daddy wilt away, Lily. It was the most traumatizing thing I had ever gone through as a child. It killed me to see my tough father like that. I'm still haunted by the visions."

"Layna is smart and strong. I promise you she'll be okay. We just have to explain things to her. You see how good she's been at taking care of me." I try to ease his mind.

"But she sees me as her super dad, Lily. She sees me as her hero."

"You'll always be her hero, Chance. Don't you know that?"

Chance shakes his head in frustration. "She's used to me running with her, protecting her, playing sports with her. Come on, Lily. You know what I mean."

"Look at me, Chance."

But he continues to stare straight ahead, avoiding me.

I drive my wheelchair so I'm right in front of him, in his field of vision. Now, he'll be forced to look at me. "Do you see me? Do you really see me, Chance?"

Chance blinks a few times, confused.

"I've lived my life in a wheelchair. How do you think I've felt my entire life? And you know what has been the worst? That I couldn't even pick up my own baby when she cried for me. I had to wait for somebody else to bring her to me. Even still, I used to be afraid that I might drop her or hurt her because my arms might move all crazy. But, no matter what, I didn't let it stop me from living. You're already signing your death certificate. Stop it! Look at Stephen Hawking. Did he give up? Did I give up?"

"But I'm not you! I've always told you that you're a lot stronger than me. You've been able to accomplish whatever you've wanted in your life. But me? I'm a coward. If I can't control a situation, I run and hide. Don't you know that? I'm not strong like you." Chance sounds desperate for me to understand.

"Believe it or not, you're the one who gave me the confidence. You made me believe. It's not that I'm stronger than you. That's such bullshit…and a copout. I've made a conscious choice. I choose strength, Chance! I choose strength."

Eventually, Chance does need a wheelchair. Luckily, the house is built so that it can accommodate both of our needs.

When Layna confronts him about all of the changes he's going through, he says, "I get tired sometimes, honey. I guess I should come clean with you. I have something called ALS, which stands for Amyotrophic Lateral Sclerosis."

"What? I've heard of ALS. What do you mean you have it?" she asks, suddenly worried.

Chance calls me over, and we both talk to Layna, explaining what it means. I'm not sure if she understands all of it, but she's clearly distressed.

"Is there a cure?"

Chance laughs. "Well, no. Not yet. It's progressive."

"Is it kind of like CP like Mom has?"

"Not exactly, honey. Well, some things can be similar. I'll be going to more therapy sessions like Mom. I may need to talk with a computer. We'll see. We can't know for sure."

"Do I have ALS?" Layna asks, her voice soft.

Chance's shoulders immediately tighten as tension builds in the room. Unable to answer, he tries to find the right words.

"When you're an adult, you can get tested for ALS if you want to find out more about it. You're a healthy young girl, though, so you don't need to worry about silly things like that," I explain to Layna since Chance is overcome with emotion.

Suddenly, a look of determination flashes in Layna's eyes. "I'm going to find a cure for ALS and CP. You wait."

Without saying another word, she sprints upstairs to her room. Knowing her, she'll be up all night researching about ALS. I sigh, accepting that she has to do what she needs to in order to understand.

Once we reach our room, Chance finally speaks. "I'm worried about her, Lily. What if she has it? I'll never be able to forgive myself."

"Are you listening to yourself? For a physician, you say some really dumb things. You can't control that. I refuse to live in fear. And, I won't allow you or Layna to live in fear. Life is too precious and too short."

"Don't tell me you're not scared!" Chance yells.

"Of course, I am. I'm scared every single day. I pray every minute of day and night that she doesn't carry the mutated gene for it. I even try to bargain with God. That's all I can do. There are some things I can't control, and I have to make the most of it. I know that whatever life throws, we'll have to deal with it. Together and as a family. There is no choice."

Chance sighs and transfers into the bed while I do the same. "I miss stretching you and massaging you, Lily. I loved touching your body and how it responded to my touch. Now, I'm useless. I can't do anything I loved."

I grab his hand and bring it to my breast. I want him right now. Who knows how long we will still be able to make love, but I'll be damned if I waste any nights without it.

Instantly, Chance responds. "Well, I guess I can still do some things I love," he whispers.

Until We Meet Again

Farewell

Chapter Twenty-eight

After Layna turns eighteen, she announces that she'd like to get the genetic testing to see if she has that same mutated gene for ALS that runs in the family. Chance is horrified, thinking it'll change the way she lives. Layna is stubborn, though, and insists that whether he agrees or not, she'll be going through with it. She's kind of like me that way. She'd rather live with the knowledge than live in ignorance.

Nothing can describe the feeling when the results come back negative.

Layna does not have that dreaded mutated gene that runs in Chance's family. I want to scream with joy at the top of my lungs. My baby doesn't have that gene that has haunted us all these years!

It feels like the heavy burden that we've been carrying all this time has suddenly been lifted. Chance literally grabs his daughter into his embrace and starts crying. Layna has never witnessed her father sobbing like this, but as she hugs him back, she cries with him. I now see the turmoil he's been going through all these years.

Besides my mom weeping, even my father is softly crying to himself in the corner.

After this news, Chance becomes a new person. Suddenly, his optimism returns. His belief in hope and faith rejuvenates. He tells me, "Lily, I'm in a real good place. All I ever wanted was for Layna to not have that terrible gene. Don't you see? Nothing matters but the fact that Layna will be fine. My prayers have been answered."

Although Chance learns to make the most out of his situation—even when he becomes mostly dependent on his wheelchair—his wish of not suffering at the end nor having his family suffer while taking care of him comes true.

Chance Brendan Ryker dies of an aneurysm at the age of fifty-seven, a year after we find out that Layna does not have the mutated gene causing ALS. One morning, he simply doesn't open his eyes. I turn toward him in bed to wake him up for work. To my horror, even as I shake him, he doesn't budge.

When my parents hear my agonizing screams, they sprint up to our room to investigate.

According to the autopsy, a ruptured aneurysm in his brain killed him. To my relief, the doctors assure me that he didn't suffer. It all happened while he was sleeping peacefully.

A part of me is grateful that God has granted him this final wish, but the other part of me dies with him. My Chance is gone. How can I possibly exist without him?

It takes all of my strength and willpower not to completely fall apart in front of Layna when she rushes home from college. She needs to draw strength from me. Her dad has been everything to her and daddy's little girl is devastated.

While we're preparing for the services, my dad hands us two envelopes. "Chance gave me these sealed envelopes about three years ago. He said to give them to you if anything should happen to him. One is for you, Lily, and the other is for Layna."

Layna snatches the envelope with her name from her grandpa and runs upstairs to the privacy of her own room. I, on the other hand, stare at my envelope. Not wanting to open it until I'm ready, I take it to my room and place it on my table. I haven't even accepted that Chance is gone, let alone read his message to me.

I contemplate going to Layna's room to check on her, but I know she needs to be alone. She needs to go through all of the emotions to heal from this tragic loss. I just have to be there for her.

Chance is buried near my sister, Layna. He has always indicated that his place is with my family. He used to joke, "Besides, I know you'd never leave your sister. You'd want to be right next to her. And, why would I want to be anywhere else but next to you?"

I feel numb during the funeral and the memorial service. People hug us and pay their respects. Many are there from his work, but I'm on autopilot and simply go through the motions. I don't even register who comes and goes or who says what. I just need all this over so I can grieve losing the love of my life on my own.

At the memorial, I don't dare say anything. It takes all the strength I possess to keep my head upright and sit tall in my wheelchair. My father and mother both give speeches about Chance.

My dad says he was the son he never had. I purposefully try not to listen too closely for fear that I'll completely fall apart. Even people from his profession and some colleagues from his medical school say kind words about Chance. When I think it's all over, suddenly, Layna stands up and walks to the podium.

"Thank you all for coming. I see how loved and respected my father truly was. Even people who haven't seen him in years are here, which truly means a lot. All of you may know that my dad was a brilliant man. I mean, he had a crazy amount of knowledge in that brain of his." There are a few chuckles. "But did you know that he was one of the kindest men I've ever known? He was my hero. Not only because of his brilliance, but because he would give his last shirt to anybody who needed it. From a very young age, my dad took care of his father. He became one of his primary caretakers while he attended school. When my grandfather lost his battle against ALS, my grandmother soon died a year later, leaving my father all alone in this world."

Layna stops, trying to compose herself. "When he left, he came to Michigan, where he met my mother. And, it was love at first sight. No matter how much my mom resisted or tried to push him away, he persisted. He never gave up on them and eventually convinced her to marry him." Layna turns to look at me. By now, my tears are rolling down my face, remembering when we first met and how he kept showing up everywhere, no matter how rude I was to him.

"He loved you so much, Mom." Layna's voice cracks. "He told me. He said he hoped that one day I find somebody to love like he loved you. He said that kind of love is once in a lifetime and many never find it. And, he's so lucky that he found you." Layna quickly wipes the tears away from her face. "I'd like to read the letter he left me. This is how amazing my father was. I, for one, am very lucky that this hero has been in my life." Layna unfolds a piece of paper. Clearing her throat, she continues.

Dear Layna,

I am so sorry that I have to leave you so soon. But, I guess it's time for me to go. Don't you worry, my precious daughter. I will be standing by your side every step of the way, through all of the ups and downs, through the happy and sad times. When you have obstacles in your path, just think of your strong daddy,

and I'll be by your side to help you get around them or clear them out of the way.
Layna, thank you for being in my life. I can't begin to tell you how much
you mean to me. I cherish every memory we've shared together.

Now that I'm gone, it's more important than ever that you and your mom
look out for each other. Your mom acts very strong in front of others. But, I know
her. She'll lock herself in her room and fall apart alone. You have each other
now, and you have to lean on one another. I want my two favorite girls to be
happy and have a wonderful life. I've been lucky because I've had the best life I
can ever hope for.

I've said this a million times, and I'll say it again. I'm so proud of you.
I can't believe all that you've accomplished. Remember to follow all your dreams.
Life is too short, baby. I want you to do all that your heart desires. My wish for
you is that you find eternal happiness like I found in your mom.

Remember, if you ever need me, all you have to do is think of me. Even
if you can't see me, trust that I'm there, guiding you and lighting the way.

Be happy, my sweet baby girl.

Love you more than life itself,
Your daddy

Layna is crying so hard by now that I don't know if the sound of the sobbing is from me or from her. I can barely catch my breath as I fall apart in front of everyone, even though I had promised that I wouldn't. My dad walks up to Layna and brings her down. She drops to her knees in front of me and while we hold each other, we share the pain of losing the one man who has meant the world to us. With our bodies shaking from the sobs, we hold one another tightly, knowing that Chance would want us to pick up the pieces and move forward.

And although losing him is killing us right now, we know that we will eventually heal. We'll heal together, with Chance guiding us each step of the way.

A full week later, I'm brave enough to read my own letter from Chance.

Hey you,

If you're reading this, then let me start by saying I'm sorry. I don't want to leave you, but I guess somebody with higher powers is saying, "Too bad." I'm going to miss you so much. You're my soul mate, Lily, and I will find you. One day, I'll find you again.

Lily, you have completed me. Completed my life. I've thanked God every day for leading me to you. You've given me so much...taught me so much. Your love, your strength, your passion, your courage, your determination. And, you've given me Layna.

You need to know that I've got important flash drives in our safe. One has all of the information about our assets and all of our accounts. Even though I'm cutting out early on you, I'm at least reassured by the fact that financially, you both will be well taken care of for a long time.

The other flash drive has access to all of the research I've done. If Layna still decides to take that path in her career, please give it to her. She's a brilliant girl. If anybody can finish what I started, it would be her.

Lily, I don't want you to cry anymore. Remember, you "choose strength." This is the time I need you to find that strength inside you and be a mother and father for Layna. I know you're more than capable of that. She's going to need you, especially right now.

I want you to be happy. Always keep that beautiful smile on your face. I love you so much. I'll always be with you, Lily. Always.

Until we meet again...

Yours eternally,
Chance

I wipe my tears with my unsteady hand. Sometimes true strength arises from our weakest point. Taking a deep breath, I choose strength once again.

Chapter Twenty-nine

I know I'm dying. Nobody knows my body better than me. Not my family, not any of the doctors. After catching a viral infection that eventually attacks my lungs, I end up with pneumonia. The doctors have tried everything. I've been in the ICU for over two weeks, connected to all sorts of tubes and the ventilator since I can't breathe on my own.

Although I can't open my eyes, I know what's happening. My parents, who are now in their seventies, have not left my side. Kathy, along with my other friends, colleagues, personal helpers, and past therapists continue to visit. Layna has taken a leave from her medical school and has flown home. Just like her daddy, she has been attending Johns Hopkins School of Medicine. She has vowed to follow her father's steps and is focusing her career in neurology. She's been studying all of the research he left for her, committed to continue working on his findings.

Even as I lie there dying, a sense of pride fulfills me. My little girl, who is now twenty-three, has grown up to be a strong, confident woman who can accomplish anything her heart desires.

I can hear the beeping of the machines around me. I can hear the soft sobbing of my mom from the corner of the room. I can feel the occasional kisses on my forehead from my dad. Most of all, I can feel Layna holding my hand.

It's not like I haven't tried, but my body just isn't strong enough to fight any longer. My family has always known my wishes. I don't want to be hooked to any artificial means to stay alive. I'm well aware that they have discussed this and need to make some tough decisions. I only hope they remember all of my wishes.

"Mom, I love you." I hear Layna whispering in my ear. "Thank you for always being my rock and inspiring me to be my best. Be at peace, Mom. Don't worry about me. I'll be okay."

I smile to myself, knowing she's going to be fine. My parents are still around, and she has a strong support group with her friends and colleagues. Kathy also has been like a second mom to Layna. Besides, she has her dad's brains, charm, and looks. And, she has my courage. I'm not at all worried about her.

I try to squeeze her hand to let her know that I hear her. I have no idea if I'm successful, but I feel her squeeze my hand tighter.

I don't fear death, for I have lived. I've lived a blissful life for fifty-six years. It hasn't been easy. No, it hasn't been easy.

But, I learned. Even with tears in my eyes, I managed to smile. Instead of worrying about my disabilities, I learned to live through my abilities. Instead of never trusting, I learned to bring down my walls for love. Instead of feeling like I wasn't perfect, I learned that I was better because I was unique. I was me.

I finally understand the purpose of my existence. It's not to be the next president or to change the world. I've lived a long, fulfilling life with people I've loved and who have loved me back. When there has been darkness, I've searched until I found a glimmer of light. I may not have changed the world, but I changed my world.

That night, I have a wonderful dream. I'm sitting in the middle of nowhere in my wheelchair. As I look around, I notice that I'm in my wheelchair in a meadow, surrounded by beautiful wildflowers. I can feel the soft breeze flowing through my hair, and I breathe in deeply the fresh, country scent.

There's a song playing far away in the distance. I strain my ear to hear the music. It's *Perfect* by Pink. I squint my eyes to see where the song is coming from. There's a girl dancing—a lovely girl with long, curly, blonde hair. She's dancing and singing the song at the top of her lungs. And, there's a dog next to her. He's barking and running around her.

"Come on, Lily. Come dance with me," she yells.

"Layna?" I whisper. I can hear my voice, speaking clearly.

A figure is walking toward me. It's a tall man with a strong build and a confident stride. I close my eyes. What's happening?

"Hey, beautiful."

I open my eyes to see Chance's beautiful face next to mine. He looks like he did when I first met him. Just like back then, he looks young and healthy, and his eyes have that familiar twinkle. He's kneeling in front of me.

Shocked, I reach forward with shaky hands to feel his face. This time, I don't have to concentrate so hard to control my arm. I can actually touch him softly and tenderly.

He closes his eyes as I continue to explore him, trying to make some sort of sense.

"Chance? Is it really you? I thought I'd never see you again." How am I talking so clearly? And, my gorgeous husband is here, in front of me. Overwhelmed with emotion, my eyes fill with unshed tears.

"You can't get rid of me that easily. Besides, I promised you I'd find you again." Chance smiles and lovingly kisses my lips. "I've missed you," he whispers. Taking my hand, he says, "Come on, somebody's been waiting a long time to see you again."

I try to drive my wheelchair, but it doesn't move.

"You won't need that here, Lily." He pulls me up to stand with a gentle tug of my hand. I glance down, and I'm standing on my feet without anybody holding me up. Astonished, I look at Chance questioningly. Chance winks at me and encourages me to take a step.

As if it's the most natural thing in the world, I step with my right foot and then the left.

Suddenly, the dog is right next to me, jumping up and down, wagging his tail. I scream in delight, "Duke!" He tackles me down and licks my face all over. "Duke, it's really you!" I laugh because I can't believe this amazing dream.

Pulling myself up, I glance ahead. Layna is laughing and still singing our song. "Well, come here, sis! We have so much to talk about."

Moving one foot after another, I break out in a full sprint toward her with Chance and Duke running by my side.

About the Author

Jalpa Williby immigrated to the United States at the tender age of eight. Faced with many obstacles in the "new country," Williby pushed herself to conquer all of the challenges. After graduating with a Bachelor's of Science from the University of Illinois, Williby went on to earn Masters in Physical Therapy from Northwestern University. Her passion of helping her patients led her to a specialty in neuroscience, focusing on children and adults with neurological impairments.

Williby's previously published novels, The Chaysing Trilogy, have won multiple awards and are Amazon best sellers. Chaysing Dreams and Chaysing Memories have been awarded gold medals from Readers' Favorite International Book Awards in Romance Suspense category. Chaysing Destiny has earned multiple five star seals.

Williby now introduces My Perfect Imperfections in hopes to educate and inspire her readers.

Website: http://jalpawilliby.com

Fan Group: www.facebook.com/groups/JalpaWilliby

Facebook: www.facebook.com/JalpaWillibyAuthor

Twitter: https://twitter.com/JalpaWilliby

Pinterest: www.pinterest.com/jalpaw

Author's Note

First and foremost, I want to thank Amanda Walker and Angie Martin for their guidance and patience. You helped keep the vision alive for My Perfect Imperfections.

I must also recognize my family for once again being patient while I buried myself into my "literary world."

My Perfect Imperfections is very dear to my heart. After years of working with my special needs friends, I can only hope that this book can do them justice. I especially want to thank all who interviewed for me to help me "get it right." I so appreciate you entrusting me with your deepest thoughts, fears, and desires.

Lastly, I would be nothing without my readers. Thank you, thank you! If you enjoyed reading this story, I would love for you to leave a review on Amazon and/or Goodreads. Your support means the world to me.

You can keep up with latest news on my novels at http://jalpawilliby.com.